THE CALL OF DUTY

Lacie Nation
Jackie M. Smith
Jean C. Joachim
Sandy Sullivan
D. F. Krieger

Erotic Romance

Secret Cravings Publishing
www.secretcravingspublishing.com

A Secret Cravings Publishing Book
Erotic Romance

The Call of Duty
Copyright © 2012 Lacie Nation, Sandy Sullivan, Jackie M. Smith, Jean Joachim, D. F. Kreiger
Print ISBN: 978-1-61885-341-7

First E-book Publication: November 2012
First Print Publication: November 2012

Cover design by Dawne Dominique
Edited by Stephanie Ballestreri
Proofread by Rene Flowers, Ariana Gaynor
All cover art and logo copyright © 2012 by Secret Cravings Publishing

ALL RIGHTS RESERVED: This literary work may not be reproduced or transmitted in any form or by any means, including electronic or photographic reproduction, in whole or in part, without express written permission.

All characters and events in this book are fictitious. Any resemblance to actual persons living or dead is strictly coincidental.

PUBLISHER
Secret Cravings Publishing
www.secretcravingspublishing.com

Dedication

This is dedicated to all of the men and women who serve in our military.

TO LOVE A SOLDIER
Lacie Nation
Copyright © 2012

Prologue

No one could've known a costume party would change lives irrevocably. Jamie had come up with a plan with her best friend, Baylee, to throw a party to welcome home Baylee's twin brother, Ethan and some of his friends. Everything about the night was supposed to be about celebrating these brave soldiers coming home from war and making their leave as memorable as possible. She had no idea what they were all in for.

Jamie drank more than she should have. But then that was the point of the party, to enjoy. Jolie and Ethan were definitely taking advantage, making out in the corner like teenagers. Somewhere along the way, Jamie had dared her best friend to have sex with a stranger. What was more surprising was Baylee actually going through with it.

She noticed one of the guys that had come with Ethan staring at her. Feeling brave, she went to him and started dancing. Before the night was through, she found herself perched on his lap and kissing him as if her life depended on it.

"I'm making out with you like I've known you for years," she said against his supple lips. "I don't even know your name."

His rich laugher vibrated against her mouth. "My name is Adam Butler."

"Well, Adam Butler, I can honestly say it's a pleasure to meet you." She brazenly swiveled her hips against him.

"You really shouldn't tease like that." His words were followed by a moan.

Jamie leaned close to his ear and whispered, "Who says I'm teasing?"

Adam pulled his head back a little to look into her eyes. She wasn't a one night stand kind of girl, but he brought things out in her she'd never felt before.

"If you're not teasing, then lead the way. I dare you." He raised an eyebrow as if waiting to see if she would follow through with her brave talking ways.

The look in his eyes caused undiluted desire to flood through her. She stood up, grabbed his hand, and led him to her bedroom.

"You look like you know how to please, Mr. Butler. Show me what you've got. I *dare* you."

Funny how a simple little word like dare would ultimately change lives forever.

Chapter One

Jamie smiled as she sat on her bed holding the letter from Adam. He had dazzled her instantly with his towering height and beautiful hazel eyes. She had never been the type of girl to fall into bed with just anyone, but she couldn't stop herself from being with him.
She could still feel his hands as they caressed her body. The way his thumb tickled her ribs as she moved on top of him still made her smile. She loved the way a simple look from him and a small smile on his perfectly kissable lips undid her completely. She never would've imagined he would still be in her life. She figured he would take what he wanted and go back to Afghanistan when his leave was up. Imagine her surprise when she pulled his letter out of the mailbox. Flipping the envelope over, she carefully opened the flap.

> Dear Jamie,
> I can't get you off my mind. Things here are bad. Everyday another soldier gets carried in on a stretcher, or worse. Even in my sleep I hear gunshots, or the unmistakable rumble of a roadside bomb. The only way I can get through the worst of days is to think about you. I know that sounds crazy because I just met you, but you touched a part of me I didn't even know existed. I have no right to ask anything of you, but will you write to me, Jamie?
> Yours truly,
> Adam

* * * *

Jamie and Adam wrote each other every day for months. With every letter she received, she loved him more. Watching Baylee, fall in love, marry, and get pregnant with the man she'd dared her friend to have sex with at the costume party, Jamie realized she wanted it all. With Adam.

Sometimes she hated reading his words because they described what he had to see every day. Adam was a medic for the U.S. Army. He saw the horrors of war because it was his job to fix what bullets and bombs ripped apart. While most of his words were poetic and told her how much he loved her, some were dark and frightening when he talked about the things he saw. His deployment was up in just a month. He would return home with Baylee's twin brother Ethan, and her husband, Nash.

"What are you thinking about?" Baylee asked as they sat on the front porch of her family's house.

"Nothing much," Jamie lied through her teeth.

She didn't want to say anything about her relationship with Adam just yet because Baylee had so much going on in her own life.

"You lie, but I won't pry."

Jamie smiled because of course her best friend would know she wasn't being honest. Baylee waddled inside to let her mother, Laura, feel the baby kick. As Jamie got up to follow her, she noticed a dark blue town car pulling down the driveway. Her heart sank to her stomach when the car was close enough for her to see the driver and passenger. They wore uniforms. Jamie barely managed to make it inside as fear gripped her hard.

"Government car in the driveway," she said in a frightened voice as she stumbled into the kitchen.

The look Baylee and Laura shared was one of dread. Everything happened so fast as the uniformed men told Laura that her son had been killed in action and Baylee's husband had been injured. All she could do was hold Baylee as tight as she could while her friend mourned her brother. Thoughts of Adam ran through her mind. Was he there? Was he injured? She had so much on her mind, her head ached.

There was nothing Jamie could do except listen while Baylee called her father to tell him of Ethan's death. When the call was done, she drove Baylee to Jolie's house, Ethan's long time girlfriend. Jamie had never seen such pain before. Jolie's unrelenting wails as she tried to deny what she was being told were enough to break Jamie's heart. As much as she wanted to be there for her friends, she really needed to hear Adam's voice. The fact she could think about anything other than Ethan being gone left Jamie riddled with guilt.

The day of the funeral, Jamie wanted nothing more than to stay in bed until the sadness was gone. She knew she couldn't though, because her friends needed her. Baylee had yet to really allow herself to feel the loss of her brother. Jolie was so far gone in her depression, Jamie worried she may never find her way out of it.

As she walked into the funeral home, she saw him. Adam. He was there, in his uniform, paying his respect to his fallen friend. Her breath caught in her throat as he slowly turned and looked at her with tormented eyes. In that moment she knew what he was thinking. She could see it in the slight furrow of his brow and the way he tried so hard to keep his emotions in check. She made sure Baylee had made it to her family before she quickly grabbed Adam by the arm and pulled him to a back room. She didn't look into the casket because she didn't think she could handle having the image of Ethan lying in there dead as her final memory of him. She wanted to remember him like he was at the party. Big, jovial, overprotective, and laughing a laugh that could make the world smile.

When she was alone with Adam, she didn't say a word. She just pulled him into her arms and held him as tight as she could. Jamie took in everything about him. His scent, the tremble of his shoulders, his heavy breathing, and the way he hesitated ever so slightly before he wrapped his arms around her and buried his face in the crook of her neck. Everything overwhelmed her, but he was here, with her.

"You're here," she finally whispered.

"I couldn't save him—" He gasped for breath and tightened his hold on her. "I tried so hard, but there was nothing I could do."

"Don't do this to yourself." Jamie didn't try to hide the tears streaming down her face. She pulled away from him and looked deep into his eyes. "I love you, Adam. I'll be here for you in any way I can."

She hadn't told him her true feeling for him in her letters because she'd wanted to tell him in person. The expression on his face was a cross between anger and awe.

"This is one of the worst days of my life, but with four words you make it bearable."

A ghost of a smile graced his lips. His eyes were still haunted, but that hint of a smile gave her hope he could get through this.

Chapter Two

Jamie woke when Adam kicked her as he thrashed around in his sleep. He was having a nightmare. She smoothed his hair trying to calm him. But as soon as her hand made contact with him, he grabbed her wrist and pinned her to the bed. His face no longer held the peaceful look she loved so much. Now, his handsome features were twisted in anguish as horror swirled in his eyes.

"Adam," she said softly so she didn't scare him anymore than he already was. "Adam, it's me. It's Jamie." His grip tightened on her wrists. "Adam, calm down baby."

Adam's face was only an inch away from hers. Her words weren't registering, so she did the only thing she could think of. She kissed him. He tensed for a moment before he returned her kiss with so much passion it made her toes curl. Jamie knew she should ask him what had happened, but as she felt the tension in his body leave, she couldn't bring herself to bring the subject back up.

"I love you Jamie," he whispered against her neck and placed open mouthed kisses on her collarbone.

This was the man she'd fallen in love with. This gentle, passionate man who worshiped her body was who she wanted to spend the rest of her life with. His hands felt like heaven on her skin. The hard plains of his body were pressed tightly against her and she could feel how hard he was for her. She rolled her hips and moaned at the friction the movement caused.

"Adam, are you sure—"

"Just love me, Jamie. Just let me love you." His words, while sweet, where laced with desperation.

Instead of pushing him away and demanding he talk to her like she probably should have, she pulled him closer until their bodies were one. He filled her up so completely he took her breath away. She moved with him in a steady rhythm and as much as she knew this wasn't helping him get past what happened in Afghanistan, she wouldn't stop giving him whatever comfort she could.

"You feel amazing," she said softly. She ran her nails lightly down his spine and smiled when he shivered.

Adam wrapped his left hand around her right ankle and guided her leg up until it rested on his shoulder. The angle caused him to sink so much deeper into her, making her cry out. Her head spun with love and passion. He sat up on his knees. The sight nearly made her eyes roll back into her head. His chiseled chest and ripped abs flexed with his movements. She could see him entering her and pulling back. Nothing had ever turned her on more than seeing him move like that. An orgasm slammed through Jamie before she even knew what was happening.

She watched as Adam's mouth dropped open, his brows pinched together and his head fell backward. He cried out her name in reverence as he pulsed inside her. He gently let her leg go as he gathered her into his arms and held her tightly. Jamie smiled as she wrapped her arms around him. Her smile fell as soon as she felt the first shudder of his strong shoulders. The shudder was followed by the sound of his teeth grinding. He swallowed hard, and then she felt a drop of moisture land on her bare shoulder. Her heart ached for him because there was nothing she could do to make it better. There was one person who might be able to talk to Adam though. Someone who had been there, someone who knew what had happened. Nash Jenson, her best friend's husband.

* * * *

Adam strolled down the isle of the barn Jamie had brought him to. He hadn't wanted to come, but she'd insisted. He learned early on to never argue with her because he would never win. He stopped midstep as a familiar voice registered. When he turned around, he saw exactly who he thought it would be. Nash Jenson. Adam stood a bit taller out of habit. Nash had been his commanding officer. Not only that, but his friend. Adam had seen the man in action and had never before met anyone with more courage. Suddenly, Adam realized why Jamie had been so insistent on brining him to the ranch.

"Sergeant Jenson," Adam said standing at attention. His actions were automatic. They had been drilled into him since the age of eighteen.

"At ease, soldier. This isn't the army." Nash held his hand out for Adam to shake. "It's been a while."

"Yes, it has." Adam hadn't seen Nash since the funeral and even then he hadn't spoken to him because he had been trying to comfort his very pregnant, grieving wife. It had been a little over three months since Ethan Crawford had been killed.

Three months of nightmares and memories trying to tear every shred of his sanity apart piece by piece. A few stalls down from where he stood, a horse kicked the door making a loud banging noise. Nash flinched, but Adam nearly dove to the ground. His heart pounded in his chest. His stomach dropped with the feeling of impending doom. His mind filled with images of thick smoke, horrified screams, and blood. Adam couldn't stop shaking. His legs wobbled and threatened to give out on him. He felt someone trying to grab at him, so he pushed them away and tried to run.

"Lieutenant! Stand strong!" The voice was deep, strong, and commanding. The tone in which the words were spoken snapped Adam out of the flashbacks and into the present.

He shook his head so he could focus. Nash stood there with a worried look on his face. To his utter horror, Jamie was on the ground looking at him with frightened eyes. She rubbed her wrist and he could already see a handprint shaped bruise starting to form. Adam knew instantly what had happened. She must've been the one trying to grab him to calm him down. He hadn't meant to hurt her.

"Jamie?" he asked as he stepped closer to her.

"I'm fine, Adam. Are you all right?" she asked in a thick voice as tears hung onto her lashes.

"I—I need some air." He hoped she could see the apology in his eyes before he rushed out of the barn.

He didn't stop walking until he reached a secluded spot near a creek. For some reason he felt a little peace. There were large rocks overlooking the water. He could remember Ethan telling him about going to the rocks and talking to his twin sister. Adam had no clue where he was going, but there couldn't be too many rocks like this sitting next to a creek on the property. After taking a seat, Adam closed his eyes and tried to calm his mind. Every since the day his squad had gotten hit and Ethan had died, he hadn't been able to forget it. A hand landed on his shoulder. Adam stiffened because he didn't want to talk to anyone.

"You don't have to talk, just listen." Nash sat down next to him. His cast had come off, but he still wore a brace on his left arm.

"How bad?" he asked.

"You totally checked out." Nash grimaced as he eased down on the rocks. "I was the same way when I first got back. It didn't matter how tired I was. As soon as I closed my eyes, the images started. I remember one night in particular. I had dozed off watching the news. I was having these horrible dreams about *that* day. I must've woken Baylee up because she was trying to calm me down. The next thing I know, I have my eight month pregnant wife pinned to the bed. I won't ever forget the look on her face."

"She looked terrified?" Adam asked. "Like I'm sure Jamie did just now in the barn."

"There was fear there, but not of me. She looked at me like she couldn't possibly love anything on this earth more than me. Like Jamie looked at you in the barn."

Adam smiled a little at the mention of her name. "She's one in a million."

"Yes, she is. Look, I'm not one for lecturing, but don't shut her out. If you don't feel like you can talk to her, you can talk to me, but don't shut Jamie out completely."

"I love her so much."

"You better, because that girl deserves the best."

Chapter Three

Jamie straightened the picture she had just hung on the wall of her new apartment. She had decided to move into her own place because Baylee and Nash needed the room for their growing family. Adam had gotten somewhat better in the time since his panic attack in the barn. He'd distanced himself from her though because he was afraid he would hurt her again. She'd tried to tell him she wasn't afraid, but it would take time for him to forgive himself for leaving the bruises on her arms. She was determined to make him see she wasn't afraid of him.

A couple hours later, there was a knock at the door as she put the finishing touches on the dinner she'd made for him. Jamie smiled as she opened the door for Adam. He wore a blue polo shirt and blue jeans. Adam always seemed to carry the weight of the world on his shoulders. When she pulled him into her embrace the tension in him seemed to ease a bit. His strong arms wrapped around her slender waist and held her tightly. She loved the feeling of his chiseled chest pressed so tightly against her.

"I missed you," she whispered against his neck.

Jamie couldn't see it, but she felt the slight scruff on his face shift as he smiled. "Something smells wonderful."

She knew he was referring to dinner, but she couldn't resist joking around. "Oh, thanks! It's this new perfume I bought."

A beat of silence passed before his rich laughter filled the air. Adam placed his hands on both of her cheeks and kissed her passionately. Jamie's knees went weak as his tongue probed her mouth. She missed this side of him so badly it hurt. When she pulled back a little, she noticed Adam's eyes seemed clearer. His face looked less lined with worry and more like the man she'd met over a year ago at the costume party.

"I missed you too by the way," he said softly as he rested his forehead against hers.

Jamie led him to the dining room where dinner was waiting on the table. She wasn't overly domestic, but growing up with Baylee and being around Laura, Baylee's mother, Jamie had learned how to cook a nice meal.

"I think we should take a trip, nothing major, just a little road trip to the beach or something." She loved the little smile that formed on his lips at her words.

"Jacksonville is only about eight hours away. They put on a killer fireworks show on the river for the fourth."

"I can talk to Laura and see if I can take some time off," Jamie said. She had a degree in accounting and did the books for the ranch. She hadn't thought it would be a full time job, but the ranch was nationally known and business was good. Keeping track of the money coming in from horse sales, breeding, and training had turned into a well paying job.

Adam nodded as he finished off his dinner.

Suddenly, Jamie was so excited she nearly knocked her chair over as she shot up and onto Adam's lap. Things had been so tense. Not only with Adam, but with Baylee as well that Jamie felt as though she hadn't been able to deal with her own pain over Ethan's death. She loved that man like a brother and missed him every damn day. The type of woman who wanted everyone else to be okay and in making sure her loved ones were on the mend emotionally, Jamie had ignored her own pain.

* * * *

Jamie stood on the beach in front of the condo she had rented with Adam. The sun was just coming up. They had gotten in the night before and she hadn't slept well. Instead of tossing and turning keeping Adam awake, she came down to the beach to watch the sun come up. She couldn't stop tears from filling her eyes. In the months since Ethan's death she unintentionally put him out of her mind. To think of him was to let pain into her heart. If she let the pain in, she was afraid it would never stop hurting.

She wasn't related to him by blood like Laura and Baylee. She wasn't completely in love with him like Jolie. She didn't serve her country with him as Adam and Nash had. Jamie felt like she was on the outskirts of the huge hole Ethan's death had blown into all their lives. How could she possibly hurt as badly as all the other people affected by his death? She couldn't answer that question. She only knew she did.

"What are you doing out here?"

She looked over her shoulder at Adam. He stood in the sand in nothing but a pair of shorts. His hair was mussed from sleep and there was a line down the side of his face from the pillow he'd slept on. In the early dawn hours and the beautiful pinks, purples, and oranges the rising sun made in the sky, he didn't look real.

"Just thinking." She was being vague, but she didn't want to say anything that would bring up bad memories for him.

"About what?"

Jamie took a deep breath and told the truth. "Ethan."

She saw the way his jaw flexed and his shoulders tensed, but he tried to hide it. "What about him?"

"Sometimes I wonder if I have the right to hurt so much over his death."

"What do you mean? Of course you have the right." Adam stepped in front of her and lifted her chin with his finger. "Talk to me, Jamie."

His words angered her. "Like you talk to me about what's going on in your head and heart?"

Adam pursed his lips and nodded.

She hadn't meant to sound so snappy, but she couldn't help it. He couldn't expect her to open her heart if he wasn't willing to do the same.

"You're right." He pulled her into his arms. "You tell me how you feel and I'll do the same."

Jamie could see the truth in his eyes. Her heart beat faster and her eyes burned as she opened her mouth to let it all out.

"Ever since he died I've been so worried about how everyone else was doing that I buried my own pain. Do you remember the day Baylee called me over to Jolie's place?"

Adam nodded.

"I've never seen anything like that before. It's like she just quit living life. She stopped eating, stopped bathing. She just stopped everything. I will never ever forget the look on her face when I walked into her room."

Her throat tightened as she remembered Jolie lying in her bed as Baylee tried to coax her into taking a shower. "Her eyes were so full of agony. The sound that she let loose was pure torture. I couldn't handle it, Adam. I've known Jolie since we were babies and I had to leave the room when she needed me the most. Instead of crying because it hurt so bad, I cleaned her house and called Laura. Ever since his death I've done everything in my power to make sure I didn't have to feel the full force of losing him."

"What makes you feel as though you don't have the right to mourn him though?"

"He wasn't my brother. He wasn't my boyfriend. I was just the annoying best friend of his sister who used to follow him around the barn."

"Jamie, did you know that when Ethan talked about his family, he included you?"

"What?"

Adam eased them down to the sand and put his arm around her shoulders. "He used to tell us all stories about things that happened back home. Crazy stories about his stepfather, or the things he and Baylee used to do together. He would tell us how he planned to ask Jolie to marry him as soon as his time was up. There was always this light in his eye when he talked about home, but there was this special laugh he had when he talked about you, Jamie."

Jamie tried to suppress the sob choking her, but she couldn't. She could hear the laugh Adam was talking about in her head as if Ethan was standing there next her.

"In his eyes, Baylee wasn't the only sister he had. After we went back, he found one of your letters to me."

"Oh, please tell me it wasn't one of the more risqué ones!"

Adam laughed and kissed her on the side of her head. "Yes, it was actually."

Jamie buried her face in Adam's neck as she laughed through her sadness. "I would've paid good money to see the look on his face."

"It was priceless! You know he was a nosy bastard, so of course he read it. I must have walked in when he got to the naughty parts because suddenly he jumped up and threw the letter down like it was on fire. When I asked him what he was doing at my bunk, he turned around and grabbed me by the shirt. I've never seen him like that before. He threatened to tear me limb from limb for corrupting his little sister."

"He called me his sister?"

"He did. When I told him how I felt about you, he made sure I knew the threat still stood if I hurt you. Once we got the territorial crap out of the way, he pretended to throw up and started shouting that his eyes were burning from the things he read in the letter."

Even though she smiled, she still couldn't shake the sadness in her heart. When she looked at Adam, she realized the sadness was for him. She could find peace in her memories of Ethan, but Adam was still living with the fact he couldn't save a man so many people loved. The constant flip flop of emotions made her tired, but she wouldn't let Adam get away with not talking to her.

"It's your turn, Adam. Talk to me."

He took a deep breath and let it out slowly. She could see the resolve in his eyes, he would tell her everything.

"What do you want to know?"

"Tell me why you scream out in your sleep. What do you see when you remember that day?"

Chapter Four

Leave it to his girl to ask the hardest questions first. Adam took a deep breath and started talking. He was never one to break a promise and he damn sure wasn't going to break one to the one person he loved more than anything else.

"I was in the vehicle toward the back of the caravan. I heard the explosion. It felt like the whole earth shook when the blast went off. I could hear men screaming for a medic even before I got out of the Humvee. I grabbed my gear and headed to the front of the convoy. There were so many injuries, but they were minor. The closer I got to front, the worse off the men were." Adam grabbed Jamie's hand because his mind filled with images from that day. "When I got to the where Ethan was, he was pulling Sergeant Jenson from the wreckage. About the time Ethan got the sergeant to cover, a sniper started firing on us."

Adam would never forget the sound of that rifle. The pop followed by a split second of silence, and then a scream for help. There was no scream from Ethan though. Adam was right next to him when he'd been hit. Ethan fell back. Nash reached for him. Adam tried to stop the blood flow, but there was nothing that could've been done. He only lasted long enough to look at Nash and tell him to "Look after Baylee." No sooner had the words left his mouth, and Ethan was gone.

"Logically, I know there was nothing I could've done to save him. All my medical training tells me the bullet did too much damage. My heart though," he said softly with a shake of his head. "My heart screams out that it should've been me."

"What?" Jamie asked sharply. "Why would—" She stopped abruptly as if she couldn't bring herself to say the words.

"Ethan had a family who loved him. He had a woman who would do anything to have him back. I was alone. My family abandoned me when I was a kid. He had everything. Why was I one of the few who survived?"

Jamie moved faster than he expected and before he could blink, she was straddling his lap and staring into his eyes with so much love, it was overwhelming. "I love you. I need you here. If you had been the one who died, where would I be?"

"Jamie—"

"No, Adam, I was here waiting for you. When they notified Ethan's family of his death, all I could think about was if you were okay or not. I cried for days. Days Adam, wondering if you were alive or dead. I don't think I took a breath until I saw you at the funeral."

He hated the tortured look in her eyes. That look would only get worse when he told her his next bit of news.

"I have to go back, Jamie." His voice was tight with guilt.

"Excuse me?"

"I'm still in the Army. I got my deployment papers the day we decided to take this trip."

Her throat bobbed as she swallowed roughly. Adam could see the absolute fear in her eyes. "How long?"

"Six months. My enlistment is up when I get stateside again."

"Will you reenlist?"

"Not if you don't want me to."

"I can't make that decision for you, baby. I know I will worry about you every single second you're gone, but that's a decision you have to make."

Adam knew he had no right to ask her to wait for him, but he couldn't leave not knowing where he stood with her. "What's this mean for us?"

She sighed and tilted her head. "It means that I had better dig out my stationary." She smiled brightly at him and it warmed his heart. "Six months is nothing, Adam. As long as you promise to come home to me, I will wait for you."

He pulled her into his arms and held her as tight as he could without hurting her. Adam never thought he would be the type of man who needed a woman in order to survive, but when Jamie gallivanted into his life, everything inside him shifted and she became his world.

"I promise to do my absolute best to come home to you." He couldn't promise her he would defiantly come home because he didn't know what the future held for him.

Jamie leaned in and whispered in his ear, "I want you, Adam."

The feel of her breath across his skin gave him chills. Her weight on his lap felt right, and the roll of her hips against him drove him crazy. Adam stood as quickly as he could while keeping a tight hold on Jamie and went inside. He didn't make it to the bedroom. Instead, he sat her on the counter. He let everything he felt flow through him as he kissed her. Jamie pushed his shorts down. When he grasped the waistband of her shorts, she lifted her hips so he could rid her of her clothes. He skimmed his fingers up her rib cage causing her to shiver. He couldn't wait a second longer to have her, so he spread her legs wider and pushed into her in one swift motion. Jamie dropped her head back and moaned his name. The sound of her voice spurred him on.

"You feel so good baby," Jamie said as she shifted her hips. The movement caused him to go deeper and it made his head spin.

"I love you, Jamie." He looked deep into her eyes when he said the words. He wanted her to know he absolutely meant it.

"I love you too."

She fit with him perfectly. Adam never wanted to leave the confines of her body, but he couldn't stop his orgasm from bursting out of him. His legs shook, his arms strained as he rested his weight on them. He let his head fall to Jamie's shoulder. Her fingers tickled the hair line at the back of his neck. She whispered soft words into his ear of how much she loved him. Adam gathered her into his arms and carried her up to the shower. He washed her hair and cleaned her body. When they finished showering, he cooked breakfast before they went to the beach. He had about four weeks before he was deployed and he planned on spending every possible moment he could with her.

Chapter Five

Jamie hugged Adam with all her might. She'd had four weeks with him and they had been blissful. She'd tried not to cry or make his leaving any harder on him than it already was, but her emotions were on the fritz and with every second she sat next to him at the airport waiting, the more she felt a fragment of her strength failing. She remembered watching Baylee say goodbye to Nash when he was deployed. Her friend had been so strong while Nash was still there. When he walked away to board his plane, Baylee had lost it. Jamie wondered if she would be the same way. She had chosen to come to the airport with Adam alone. She didn't want to share him with anyone.

"I have to go to the gate now," Adam said in a tight voice.

"We can handle six months." She wasn't sure if she was trying to comfort him or herself.

"I love you, Jamie."

"I love you too, Adam, and I'll be here when you come home."

He wrapped his arms around her and lifted her feet off the ground. Jamie smiled against his neck and breathed in deep. She wanted to remember his smell and the feel of his body pressed tightly against hers. Sadly, Adam pulled away, placed a kiss on her lips, and then rested his forehead against hers.

"I don't want to leave you."

"The faster you leave, the faster you can come home."

Adam laughed at her logic. "Are you in a hurry to be rid of me?"

"Absolutely," she said with a wicked little smile on her face.

"You wound me with your words."

Jamie grew serious then. "You know I don't want you to go. If you stand here with me much longer, I will start to get overly emotional and all girlie on you."

"Oh, the horror!" His ability to understand her humor and give it back tenfold was yet another reason she loved him so much.

A moment later, he placed her on her feet, kissed her forehead, and turned to leave. He looked back and winked at her over his shoulder before he disappeared through security. He looked so strong in his uniform. When he finally faded from her field of vision, she felt like her chest was being squeezed in a vice grip. Her heart pounded, her mouth went dry, and her eyes burned like there was acid in them. She had to back up against the wall so she didn't fall down. Jamie eased down into a squatting position and wrapped her arms around her legs. A moment later, she felt someone touch her head. When she looked up, she saw Baylee there.

"What are you doing here?"

"I thought you could use a friend."

"He's been gone less than five minutes and I miss him so much it hurts."

"I know it hurts. It will get easier though."

"How?"

"You lean on your family. Do the same things you always do. Live your life and before you know it, he'll be home."

Baylee held her hand out. Jamie accepted, allowing Baylee to help her up. When she was standing, Baylee pulled her into her arms. Jamie could no longer hold in her tears, or the gut wrenching sobs. She held onto her best friend in the middle of the damn airport for who knows how long. When she felt calm enough to move, she walked with Baylee outside.

"Where'd you park?" Jamie asked.

"I had Nash drop me off. He's got all three of the kids today."

"Poor man. Are the twins on any kind of a schedule yet?"

"Yes, they have somehow scheduled themselves to eat, sleep, or anything else that requires a moderate amount of energy on our parts at completely opposite times."

"You snagged yourself a pretty good man, you know that, Baylee?"

"Yeah, I think I'll keep him. I have you to thank for giving me the push."

Jamie huffed a breath across her fingernails and polished them on her shirt causing Baylee to laugh. "Seriously though, I only dared you to have sex with him. You're the one who made it work."

Baylee tossed her arm around Jamie's shoulder as the two women walked to Jamie's car. Jamie was thankful Baylee cared enough to come to the airport. She didn't think she would've gotten through the day without her friend. Now, if she could just keep Baylee glued to her side for the next six months, she might stand a chance of not going insane without Adam.

* * * *

Adam had been gone for a month. Jamie hung out at Baylee and Nash's more than she stayed at home because she couldn't handle being alone. She loved how the chaos of the Jenson household kept her mind off things. Baylee's children were beautiful, but an absolute handful. The twins were growing so fast and kept Baylee and Nash busy constantly. Baby Ethan, named after his uncle, was a great big brother as long as it didn't require him to share his mommy.

"Jamie, could you help me for a minute?" Baylee asked from the twins' room.

When Jamie walked into what used to be her room, she couldn't help but laugh. Summer was bouncing in her crib, dirty diaper in hand, her twin brother had spit up all over Baylee, and baby Ethan had the baby powder. The smart little man had learned that if he squeezed the bottle, powder would shoot out of the lid.

"Oh, wow. So this is your life?"

"Honey, this is just the tip of the iceberg. Please grab Summer before she—"

"I'm on it!" A baby without a diaper was a disaster waiting to happen. "Hey sweet girl! Let's get you cleaned up."

Jamie threw the diaper away, then grabbed Summer and took her to the bathroom to give her a bath. As she bathed her goddaughter, she wondered if she and Adam would ever have a family. She could envision the full picture with him and she wanted it badly.

"How's it looking in here?" Baylee asked as she brought in a freshly cleaned Tyler and Ethan.

"We're good." Jamie drained the water and wrapped a towel around Summer.

Jamie helped Baylee get all the babies dressed and ready for the day. They took the kids to Laura's house before they headed down to the barn. Baylee had a few horses to train, Nash would help her. Jamie headed into her office and submerged herself in paperwork. No matter how busy she kept herself, Adam was always at the forefront of her mind. She wondered what he was doing at that moment. Was he safe? Did he think of her?

"Jamie?" Jolie asked from the doorway.

Jamie hadn't seen Jolie in quite a while. The last time she'd seen her was at the hospital when the twins were born.

"Jolie!" Jamie jumped up, ran to her, and pulled Jolie into her arms. "Where have you been?"

"I went and stayed with my mom in Atlanta."

"How is she?"

"She's good. The time away was good for me."

"How are you doing?" Jamie asked softly.

"Some days are better than others, but I'm getting through it. I went to the cemetery yesterday. Still makes my heart hurt." Jolie shook her head as if to rid herself of the emotion she was fighting. "So, tell me about your guy."

Jamie smiled at the mention of Adam. "He's wonderful. We decided to move in together when he gets home."

"Is this the guy you were all over at the costume party?"

Jamie laughed. "Yes, we've been together ever since then. I never thought I would be the type of girl who would jump in with both feet, but with him, I can't help it."

She wondered if it was hard for Jolie to hear about other people's happiness when her first and only love was gone. Suddenly, Jamie felt guilty, all consuming guilt for being so happy when Jolie was barely climbing out of her pain. Tears blurred her vision and her throat felt so tight she couldn't breathe.

"Hey, hey, Jamie, don't do that. Don't feel guilty for being happy." Jolie pulled Jamie into her arms.

"How did you know?"

"Ethan's been gone over a year now, Jamie. I know that look. Anytime someone smiles around me they immediately get that look. They act like I'm going to fall completely apart because they're happy."

Jolie sounded a little angry about that, so Jamie took a deep breath and calmed down. "I'm sorry. I just don't know what's okay to talk about and what's not. I don't want to add anymore heartache to your life Jolie, you've been through enough."

"See, here's the thing," Jolie said as she led Jamie to the chairs in the corner. "I loved that man more than anything in the world. He was everything to me and he died. When I found out what had happened, none of it seemed real. When I realized he really wasn't coming home, I had to learn how to live again. When people think I'm not capable of hearing about the goodness in their lives, how do you think that makes me feel?"

"I'm sorry. It just hit me out of nowhere. You have to know I would never intentionally make you feel bad."

"Hearing about your happiness, Baylee's happiness, it makes me smile because I know Ethan is watching over us all. I miss him every day, but I have to believe he's always with me."

"You know he is. But you also know he'd want you to move on with your life."

"I will, when it's right for me. I spent my whole life with him. I can't just close that book and open another. I have to learn how to live life on my own first."

Jamie could see the strength in Jolie's eyes, but she knew her friend wasn't completely over the loss of Ethan. Perhaps she never would be.

"Surprisingly, it helps to hear how great my loved one's lives are." Jolie smiled and winked at Jamie. "So, tell me all about Adam."

Jamie did just that. She told Jolie everything about Adam. Every tiny detail she could think of, Jamie shared with her. The way he laughed at all her stupid jokes. The way his eyes sparkled when he smiled at her. How she felt so incredibly safe when his arms were around her. Most of all, she told Jolie about how scared she was that he wouldn't come back from this deployment.

"You can't think like that, Jamie. If you put yourself through that, it will drive you crazy. You have to know in your heart he will come home to you."

"He wouldn't actually say the words 'I promise to come home.'"

"Because he can't make a promise to you he may not be able to keep. Let me guess, he promised he'd do his best to make it home."

"Yes, in those exact words."

"I used to hate when Ethan would say that to me. Now I understand why though. He knew how much harder it would've been had he promised to come home. On top of the pain of losing him, I would've been so angry."

"But weren't you angry?"

"Of course I was, but not at Ethan. I knew what it was to love a soldier. I knew the danger of loving him when he was deployed. I chose to love him and even though his death nearly killed me, I wouldn't change a second of time I had with him for anything in the world."

"How can you talk about Ethan and not fall completely apart? Not that I'm not proud of you for healing, but it still guts me to think about him."

"There will never be a day when it doesn't hurt unbelievably bad to think or talk about him, but I know the world would be a darker place if he wasn't talked about. To never speak of him again because it hurts too badly would be the ultimate disrespect to his memory."

Jamie nodded. If Jolie could talk about Ethan, remember him, and not fall apart every time he came to mind, then so could she. She would get through these next five months and welcome Adam home with open arms.

"Thank you," Jamie said laying her head on Jolie's shoulder.

"For what?"

"For being you."

Jolie laughed. The sound was something Jamie hadn't heard in such a long time. She was so happy her friend was back. She wouldn't ever be the same, but her strength and ability to help others through whatever they were going through, would always be there.

"Ladies, I think we need to go ride," Baylee chimed as she entered the office.

Jamie hadn't ridden in so long. She realized she could use the time with her friends. After the three of them saddled up their horses, they made for the trails. August heat was blistering, and the humidity horrible, but she wasn't complaining, for once, she wasn't thinking about anything sad. The wind in her hair, and heavy blowing of her horse's breath helped her find a sense of peace as the raced along the hills.

At home that evening, she wrote Adam a letter to tell him about her day. He wouldn't get it for weeks, but she wanted to share things with him when they happened.

> *Dear Adam,*
> *I miss you every day. I stayed with Baylee last night because sometimes being here without you hurts too much. I helped her with the kids this morning. They are so innocent and trusting. I've never seen someone as happy in the midst of such chaos as Baylee is. I want that someday...with you.*
> *Jolie was at the barn today. She laughed and there was a realness to it I didn't think she'd ever feel again. She's one of the strongest women I know. I was on the verge of losing it because I missed you so bad and she talked me through it. She said to love a soldier was one of the hardest things to do. It takes a special kind of woman to handle this life and all it brings. While I can't say talking with her took away all my fears and sadness, it did help me understand it all. Baylee, Jolie, and I went riding on the trails today. I'd forgotten how much it helps to just let go and trust the horse to take it all away. Maybe when you get home, we can take a ride together.*
> *I hope this letter finds you well. I'm counting down the days until you are in my arms again. I love you, Adam, so very much. Hope to hear from you soon, baby.*
> *Love Always,*
> *Jamie*

Chapter Six

Jamie crossed off another day. Three months down, three to go. She could do this. Letters were all well and good, hearing his voice on the phone when he was able to call was better, but nothing would ever compare to being in Adam's arms. She never imagined feeling the way she did for him. Every single beat of her heart was for him. Jamie had always been an independent woman and still considered herself to be that way, but she could still be strong and need Adam at the same time.

"Jamie, are you ready?" Baylee asked.

Tonight was Thanksgiving dinner at Laura's. Every year there was a huge get-together at the ranch house. Laura and her husband, Mark cooked massive amounts of food and invited everyone over. She didn't really feel like going because she didn't think she could handle seeing Baylee and Nash together without getting down about Adam being stuck in the desert alone during the holidays.

"Would it be horrible if I just stayed home?"

"Yes, now get your ass in the car."

Baylee grabbed Jamie's arm and literally pulled her from the apartment and actually put her in the car. Jamie never got the chance to protest before Baylee took off to her mother's house.

"Guess I'm going."

"Three months will go by in a flash, Jamie. Sitting at home moping about his deployment won't bring him back any faster."

"I know it's just so hard. I miss him so much."

"I know you do, but he'll be home soon."

Baylee smiled as she drove. "Why are you so happy? Are you pregnant again?"

"Lord no! I think three kids is enough. I'm happy because I love it when we all get together. Last year was so sad because it was the first Thanksgiving without Ethan. I hope this year will be better."

Whenever Baylee talked about Ethan, darkness clouded her eyes. Even though she had dealt with her pain over his death,

Jamie didn't think Baylee would ever really be able to let it go completely. The rest of the drive was quiet. When they arrived, she noticed they were the last ones there. As soon as Jamie opened the car door she could smell the wonderful aroma of all the traditional Thanksgiving foods Laura and Mark had prepared. Her stomach rumbled in anticipation.

She followed Baylee into the house where she saw Nash in the living room trying to corral the three babies. Baby Ethan was walking around Nash's legs while Summer and Tyler were crawling behind him. There wasn't an irritated molecule in his body. The man was truly happy to be in that moment with his children. When he looked up and saw Baylee, Jamie swore she saw stars in his eyes. She never understood the love Baylee and Nash shared until she allowed herself to really let Adam into her heart.

"Jambie!" Ethan shouted when he saw her.

Jamie laughed at the way he pronounced her name. The toddler ran into her arms and squeezed her neck tightly. Little Ethan was the spitting image of his uncle. When the boy laughed, she could swear he was a small version of the man he was named after. She put Ethan down, and then kissed the twins on the head. She hugged Nash before she went into the kitchen where Laura was putting the final touches on dinner.

"What can I help with?" she asked as she dipped her finger into the mashed potatoes. No one made mashed potatoes like Laura Hutchins.

"Jamie!" Laura stopped what she was doing, came around the island, and hugged Jamie tightly. Jamie immediately relaxed and sighed, the only thing better than her potatoes were her hugs. "I'm so glad you're here."

When Jamie parted from Laura, Jolie hugged her next. "Why is everyone in such a hugging mood today?" Jamie laughed even though she found it strange.

"Must be the holidays," Jolie said as she busied herself with grabbing the plates to set the table.

Jamie grabbed half the plates from the stack before Jolie dropped them. She walked into the dining room and started setting the table. When she set the last plate down, she turned to go back to the kitchen and ran straight into a uniformed chest. Her breath caught in her throat as she looked up and saw Adam's smiling face. Her eyes filled with tears, and her heart pounded in her chest. She reached up and touched his cheek with her fingertips just to make sure he was really standing in front of her.

"You're really here?" she barely whispered through the lump in her throat.

"Yeah, baby, I'm really here."

Oh, God, his voice is hypnotic. Only hearing it over the phone did it absolutely no justice at all. A split second went by where she couldn't move, couldn't speak, she couldn't do a single thing except stare at his ruggedly handsome face. Her body moved on its own accord as she threw her arms around his neck. His arms went around her waist and pulled her even closer as he stood straight causing her feet to leave the floor.

He buried his face in the crook of her neck as he spoke in a soft voice, "I missed you so much, Jamie."

Jamie let the sob she'd been keeping in, go. She melted against him, holding him for a long time. Finally, he set her on her feet, placed his hands on her both sides of her jaw, and kissed her lightly on the lips. No probing with his tongue, their lips were barely open, but it was the most loving kiss she had ever experienced.

"How the hell are you here?" she asked when they parted.

For the first time since seeing him, she noticed everyone else in the room. Baylee and Nash were smiling, Laura's eyes were a little misty, but what made her laugh was seeing Mark pass Jolie a ten dollar bill. They made bets with each other on every single thing they possibly could.

"I told you Jamie would cry," Jolie said proudly.

"She's always been so tough. Guess love made her soft," Mark said jovially.

Jamie took a moment to really look at Adam. His uniform fit him perfectly and the sight made her mouth water. She wanted nothing more than to peel every single article of clothing from his body, but there were eight sets of eyes glued to them and three of them were children. She would have to behave herself until she got him home.

"How long are you here for?"

Adam leaned in and whispered, "I'm home for good."

"What?" she shrieked.

"My unit's deployment was cut short. The rest of my career will be spent here in the states training new recruits."

Jamie couldn't say anything at all. All day she'd been so depressed because she had to wait another three damn months for his return. Now, he was standing right next to her with his arms wrapped around her shoulders. When she was finally able to move, dinner started. Everyone seemed like they were floating on cloud nine, but none of them were flying as high in happiness as Jamie.

She enjoyed the food and the company, but as soon as they finished eating and socialized a little, Jamie dragged Adam from the Hutchins's house and into the car. She didn't care that it was Baylee's car she took, she could ride home with Nash. Jamie drove as quickly as she dared and when they pulled into the parking lot of her apartment building, she still didn't slow down until they were inside and she was wrapped around him.

"Please don't ever leave me again," she whispered against the skin of his neck.

"I'm here, baby. I'm right here and I'm not going anywhere."

The sound of his voice, the feel of his body pressed against hers, and the way his arms held her so securely came really close to overwhelming her. She held it together though as she led him to the bedroom. He had to help her remove his uniform because her hands were shaking so badly. He eased her clothes off her body gently. Every time a piece of material glided over her skin, it left goose bumps in its wake. He lifted her into his arms and laid her on the bed as if she were a piece of valuable china. Starting at her foot, he placed soft kisses all the way up her body and didn't stop until he reached her mouth.

"I love you, Jamie." With those words, he pushed into her.

Jamie wrapped her legs around his waist and matched his movements. Having him here with her like this and being able to feel the love he had for her, sent her over the edge, plunging into bliss faster than she thought possible. He loved her tenderly and passionately. His hands gripped her hips tightly as he pulled her even closer. Jamie didn't know two people could be this connected, but with Adam, she felt as though she was a part of him. She loved the way he pulsed and cried out her name when his pleasure took him. A few moments later, he shifted to the side so he wouldn't crush her.

She lay on her right side facing him while he lay on his left and held her close, so close his forehead touched hers.

His beautiful hazel eyes gazed into hers as he spoke softly. "I want you to be my wife, Jamie. Will you marry me?"

"Yes, absolutely!"

There was nothing to think about because she had known since the beginning Adam would be the one she spent her life with. She knew there would be trying times. He would reenlist in the Army because it was all he'd ever wanted to do and she wouldn't be the one to ask him to walk away from his dreams. To love a soldier took guts and she had that in spades. The man beside her would lift her up when she was down, he would be there through the hard times and the happiest of times. Adam was her soldier, her love, her heart, and she was made to love her soldier.

The End

HEALING HEARTS

Jackie M. Smith

Copyright © 2012

Chapter One

France, September 1916

Only the sound of the engine in his Nieuport resounded around him.

Jack Cassidy never imagined a year earlier that he would be in France, flying the latest French airplane model. When he decided to leave his ranch in Texas, Jack wanted adventure and to help out the French people who suffered at the hands of the German army. The Huns had invaded France and its northern villages for the last two years, and no one saw an end to the bloodshed and horror. As for his maiden journey across the Atlantic, Jack found it too long, especially with the German submarine presence threatening to sink them. But with the grace of God, he made it to France in time for his training.

After countless missions during the last several weeks, Jack found a passion for flying and the country he had never visited before. If only circumstances were different, and he wasn't about to fight against the German squadron soon to appear in the clear morning sky above him. The other pilots depended on him to lead them toward another victory against the enemy. No one knew how this mission would end, but they needed to stop the Huns from attacking a nearby village below.

Dammit! Where did they go? He scanned the horizon. Their commanding officer, Captain Georges Thénault, had informed him and his squadron enemy planes would be in the area this morning. Maybe they changed their plans and decided to attack later. Jack let out a low groan, hoping for the opposite. He wanted to fight them and get closer to ending this bloody war. Too many of his friends had died defending themselves and innocent people on the ground.

Adjusting his goggles, he lifted his head. "There you are, you bastards!"

Jack spotted the first enemy plane coming toward him at full speed. Adrenaline made his blood pump hard. He loved fighting the enemy and making them pay for all the damage and death they had caused for the last two years. At least here in his plane, he was protected against lice and disease the men in the trenches below suffered every single day. He looked on his right and his left, making sure his fellow pilots followed his lead and were ready to confront the enemy. He gave a short nod, signaling the start of combat. Guiding his plane, he aimed the nose toward the first enemy plane and shot the first round of bullets.

"Gotcha!" He smiled, happy he shot down the plane with ease.

Another plane approached and shot at him, but Jack swerved and shot back, hitting his mark straight on. He counted two others coming his way. He stilled and said a silent prayer, waiting for them to come a little closer. With some good shots, he took down the planes. But more surrounded him and spat out their bullets against his cockpit. He let out a low groan as he reposted and maneuvered in order to get the upper hand. But as soon as he got away, another enemy plane attacked him. "God, please help me."

Jack took a quick glance at one side and then the other, hoping to see his fellow pilots. He had no idea if and how many of them had been shot down. All he could do was pray for them and for himself while a bullet pierced through his right wing. He turned his head and saw the gaping hole. Another bullet whizzed through the air making another hole through the canvas in his cockpit.

A searing pain centered in his shoulder. He squeezed his eyes for a moment and swore under his breath. Was this the way he would die? No, not today, he told himself. Not like this. Guiding his way downward as best he could, he held his breath and hoped he could reach the wide open field he spotted from the air without crashing. A gust of wind caught under his wings. He lost control and hit the ground with a thump, knocking him out.

* * * *

Commotion in the hallway caught Elodie Paradis's attention. She stopped reading her book to see what was going on.

Another batch of wounded soldiers arrived from the front. Every day, since the war began two years ago in her country, ambulances filled the hospital's yard, bringing in wounded French soldiers. Some of them barely survived, dying before they reached the hospital. Others they could save, but needed great care. Elodie stood from her desk and rushed down the hallway. These men needed her help, especially the first French soldier she examined. She froze, seeing blood and dirt covering his face and soaking his torn uniform. *What happened to him?* She took one last glance at his wounded shoulder and stomach. Blood spewed under the thick bandages.

"Get this one into surgery right now," she gently ordered the gurney.

The young man nodded.

Elodie examined the other soldiers while her fellow nurses did the same until they had no more left in the yard. She wiped her hands on a rag and took a deep breath of the fresh air before the bile in her stomach reached her throat. If only this war would end soon. Too many people suffered because of it.

Families in Paris had escaped to the country so they could feed their children and stay safe until the end of this bloody war. Unshed tears stung Elodie's eyes, thinking of her own family who had left the city months ago. She had decided to stay to help at the hospital. It was her only way to join in the war effort. For the last two years, she had seen her share of death and pain come through the hospital doors.

But she knew no amount of care would fully heal the deep cuts inside the soldiers' souls. They may never heal no matter how much care she gave them. The head nurse, Madame Valmont always reminded her she had done her best. But she hated seeing those innocent men without a smile on their face or hope in their eyes.

"*Viens*, Elodie," her friend Françoise said. "Come. We need to give the patients their medication and clean their bandages."

She nodded and followed her into the large room where the other nurses busied themselves with helping the soldiers in the beds lined against the wall on each side.

The late afternoon sun shone through the lace curtained windows, giving an eerie glow to the room. Screams resounded around her as the other nurses began to help the soldiers settle in their beds. Her heart sank deep. All these brave men suffered from their injuries and the horrors they saw only hours before. Elodie hurried down the row and filled her tray with the pain medication needed for the wounded. Thanks to medical advancements in the last months, they had more means to help the patients relieve some pain, and it will help them calm down so they may heal, she hoped. As she gave the first soldier his pain medication, he grabbed her arm.

"Please, help me. I don't want to die."

Elodie laid a hand upon his. "I won't let you die." She set the tray on the cart and helped the man lie back down. "Here you go. This will help you feel better." She gave him a pill and lifted his head so he could drink some water. "There. Rest now."

He nodded. "*Merci, ma belle.*"

She gave him a reassuring smile and went on to the next patient. When she reached the last one, she stilled. A long thin scar crossed his left cheek. His leg and shoulder were wrapped in wide bandages. *How did he suffer his wounds?* She examined the rest of his handsome face. He had no dog tags attached around his neck, no identity whatsoever. She caught herself staring at him, almost forgetting where she was.

"We must get his arm into a cast at once," the head nurse spoke behind her.

Elodie turned and nodded. "Yes, madame." She stepped away and prepared the concoction for a plaster cast.

The soldier's handsome face bounced in her tired head. If only he could speak so he could let her know if he was in pain. It would also help if she knew his name. She looked over her shoulder and saw he hadn't woke. The sun coming through the window lit up his face. Why couldn't she stop staring at him?

She shook her head and finished preparing the plaster. When she was satisfied with its consistency, Elodie returned to the unknown soldier. She stood beside him and gently prepared his arm for the cast. He had no identifiable markings, nothing to give her clues about him or where he came from. Gently, she wrapped his strong arm with more bandages while holding his warm hand. Her heart gave a start when his long, lean fingers entwined with hers. She froze as images of him holding her tight appeared in her mind, causing a stirring in her depths. She looked at him again, making a mental note of this handsome stranger. He stirred again, but he didn't wake. Before she lost herself in the moment, Elodie returned her attention to her duties before the doctor or the head nurse noticed.

"Who are you?" she asked in silence.

Elodie finished casting his arm and stretched her weary back, wishing for her bed after a long day. She pulled out her mother's pocket watch and noticed the late hour. Before she went to get some fresh air, she took one last look at her patients, making sure they were comfortable for the night. She touched the handsome unknown patient's bandaged arm and whispered, "You're safe now."

* * * *

A thick mist surrounded Jack. The early morning sun pierced through the haze hovering over the field. He scanned the horizon, but saw no one. Where was he? There were no familiar markings in sight. He wanted to move, but his legs didn't budge an inch. Looking down, he noticed his feet stuck in thick bloody mud. Dammit! He couldn't move. He was alone, and nobody was around to help him. He squeezed his eyes shut and let the cool breeze caress his cheeks.

"Jack," an unfamiliar feminine voice called out to him.

Jack opened his eyes and saw the woman who had haunted his dreams since the day he arrived in France. He didn't know her but her sweet face made him smile and gave him strength to continue fighting in the war. He reached out to her. She took a step closer. The faint sunrays caused an ethereal glow around her. Her long auburn hair cascaded down her back. If only he could touch her and hold her in his arms. His body ached for her. All his blood rushed to his groin at the sight of his fantasy. One more step and she stood a mere breath away. He could almost touch her. A hint of lavender teased his nose. He smiled, memorizing her sweet scent so he could remember her forever.

"I'm here for you, Jack. Always. Please wake up. Don't be afraid."

Consciousness gently brought him back to reality. Searing pain in his shoulder and leg made him open his eyes. He reached over and touched the thick bandages covering his skin. Heaviness in his arm made his curse under his breath. *What happened to me?* He couldn't remember. His head throbbed. *Dammit!*

"Don't move, monsieur," the familiar voice from his dreams gently ordered.

Jack stilled and looked at the young woman standing beside him. He swore he was seeing an angel. *Are my eyes playing tricks on me? Have I died?* Staring at her sweet face made him forget his pain and injuries.

She touched his hand and gave him a reassuring smile. "You mustn't move."

"Where am I? What happened?"

"Do you remember anything?"

He shook his head. He pressed his good hand to his forehead, forcing himself to recall something, anything. But everything was blurry. Only pieces of the puzzle appeared behind his closed eyes. Fear and anger twisted his gut. Taking her fingers gently in his, he said, "Please tell me where I am, why I'm here."

"You are in a hospital outside Paris, monsieur. The ambulance brought you in from the field where a farmer found you. Do you remember this?"

Again, he shook his head and let out a low groan. He leaned his weary head back against the pillow and closed his eyes. "Why can't I recall anything?"

She patted his hand. "That's all right. You will remember soon."

He turned his head and looked at her. "Thank you, mademoiselle. May I know your name?"

Her rosy lips curled upward. "Elodie."

"You're French, right?"

"*Oui*, monsieur." She giggled. "Can you tell me your name?"

"Cassidy. Jack Cassidy," he replied happily. At least he hadn't lost all of his memory. He forced his mind to remember other things about himself, but it had brought him back to his dream. Elodie was definitely the woman who had haunted them for as long as he could remember. Now, she had a name.

"It is nice to me you, Jack Cassidy," she said with her charming French accent.

Jack couldn't help the smile on his lips. "It's nice to meet you, too, Elodie."

As she moved beside him, fixing his pillow, hints of lavender reached his nose and wrapped him like a warm blanket. Her scent reminded him of his short stay in Provence during the summer. A trip he would remember forever, he promised himself. His superior officer had allowed him a few days away from the war for rest and relaxation between missions. George Thénault told him he had deserved the break after countless hours in his plane, successfully shooting down the enemy. Some of his French friends had recommended a quick trip to Provence. There, he stayed at a quaint hotel and visited the town and the nearby lavender fields. Back home, they didn't know about this flower except what they learned in schoolbooks. He had never known of its existence either until the moment he went to the French region. For as long as he lived, the heavenly scent would stay in his memory. He thought he had forgotten it until this moment.

Elodie looked at him, and their eyes locked. Jack felt his groin tighten more and hoped she didn't see his growing hardness under the blankets. Her amber eyes glittered in the light of the oil lamp on the side table. He stilled, making a mental image of the woman of his dreams. Now he knew her name. But was her heart free? Did another man love her? Panic filled him. He squeezed his eyes and concentrated on calming himself.

Again, his shoulder caused his breath to shorten. The pain was unbearable. He forced his mind to recall how he injured himself. Why had he blocked the accident from his mind? Flashes of a plane rushing toward him and loud noises rushed into his head, but he couldn't concentrate on one single image. His stomach churned.

"Are you all right?" she asked, concerned, touching his cheeks as if checking him for a fever.

He stilled, reveling in her touch. Her small hands against his skin caused his body to heat up once more. Desire rippled through him. She made him forget his pain. He looked at her and nodded, deciding if he should ask her if she did have someone in her life. *This is madness. We barely know each other for Christ's sake.* He squeezed his eyes shut, and hoped his need to touch Elodie and hold her would diminish.

"Try to get some sleep. I'll be here if you need anything."

"Thank you," he said, holding her small hand.

She gave him a smile and walked away. Jack watched her soft feminine curves under her long crisp white dress and felt another stirring within his groin. He couldn't remember the last time he felt so strongly for a woman. Back home, with his many duties at the family ranch, he had no time for love or any romantic relationship. Some of the girls near his home showed interest—some more than others, he remembered with a chuckle. When he heard about the Lafayette Escadrille on the news reel in town, he jumped at the opportunity. It was his chance to help with the war effort in France. The local sheriff told him the French were recruiting volunteers in America. Jack didn't hesitate one moment. He had no parents to care for. As for his ranch, his Uncle Sam promised to take care of it and his cattle until his return. Nothing and no one held him back. Adventure called him and he answered. He had arrived in France a week later, and headed to the front for intense training as a pilot. The only flying he had done before was some crop dusting. Flying a plane while shooting at the enemy was not an easy task. But with time and practice, he earned experience and was considered amongst the best, he recalled with pride.

Jack glanced at Elodie. His lips curled upward. Her heart-shaped face, small nose, full rosy lips—he liked everything about her. Even her silver round-framed spectacles resting on the tip of her nose appealed to him. He couldn't explain why his heart raced every time she moved. Maybe the pain medication they gave him made his head spin and his heart react that way. He didn't care. He could stare at her lovely face for hours. And he did so until his eyelids weighed down with fatigue.

* * * *

"How are you feeling this morning?" Elodie asked Jack while she held his wrist in her hand to check his heart rate.

"Better, thank you."

Elodie felt Jack's stare on her, and turned her head. Her cheeks warmed and her whole body radiated with heat. Their eyes locked in some magical force she couldn't— didn't want to pull away from. *Heaven help me!* Everything around them faded in the background. Only the beating of her heart resounded in her ears. Her head screamed, *pull away!* But she didn't listen. Instead, she stared at his mouth and imagined it upon hers, tasting, tempting. She bit her lower lip and took a step back before she lost herself forever to this man she would never see again once he left the hospital.

"Please forgive me. I must return to my duties." She gently pulled her hand away and gave him a reassuring smile. "I'll check on you later."

Elodie walked out of the room and found a quiet place on the balcony leading to the gardens. The fresh air helped to clear her fuzzy head. She let out a deep breath and willed her heart to stop racing. Why did she let Jack Cassidy touch her for such a long moment? No man had touched her since her fiancé. The day Gaston died on the front, she swore to love no one else. She had suffered enough pain for a lifetime. When she had promised herself to him, she never thought about a life without him. Now, he was gone. Unshed tears stung her eyes. She rubbed her arms against the early morning chill.

The clear blue sky gave way to some thick clouds. *Will it rain or snow today?* Autumn had always been her favorite season. In the yard, the trees gradually changed colors and soon they would sleep for the winter. She hoped this would be the last season of war. Too much blood had spewed on her homeland. Thanks to the airplanes flying over Paris, they were fairly safe from the German army, but famine and illness still threatened them.

"Are you all right, dear?"

Elodie turned and gave her friend Isabelle a reassuring smile. She nodded, wiping at her wet cheek. "I needed some air."

"If you need to talk, I'm here."

"Thank you." Elodie knew she could confide her thoughts to her friend.

Isabelle had always been there for her, especially when she learned the devastating news about her fiancé. With her family away in the country, Elodie thought her world had crumbled under her feet. She thanked the heavens Isabelle lent her a shoulder to cry on. In the months since they met, they had become best friends. They not only worked together, but stayed in the same boarding house. Isabelle knew everything about her, and she knew everything about her friend. Should she tell her friend about her reaction to Jack Cassidy? No, she reasoned.

Besides, there was nothing to say. She must push away her growing desire for him. She must stop imagining his lips against hers. Closing her eyes, the image of Jack's handsome face appeared. A honeyed sensation pulsed through her. She shook her head, chasing away the longing for a man she would never see again once he left her care.

"Do you think this war will ever end?" Isabelle asked, looking at an invisible spot on the horizon.

"I hope so," Elodie said, feeling her heart sink. Too many people she knew had disappeared from her life in such a short time. Jack would be next. Sadness invaded her, and she didn't understand the reason why. A chilly breeze whipped her face. More clouds rolled in, covering the sun. The first raindrop escaped from the thick haze above. "Let's get inside before we get wet."

More drops fell as they reached the door. Elodie turned and watched the rain drench the backyard. Again, her thoughts went to Jack. She couldn't stop imagining his arms around her, holding her, showering her with kisses. As the rain poured, she could almost see them walking under an umbrella and sharing a moment of passion and love. She couldn't remember one similar time with her fiancé. They loved each other and wanted to spend their lives together, but Gaston was never the passionate man—not like she had read in her romance books or seen with other lovers in the city. She never complained because he loved her with all his heart. Now she wondered if Jack was a passionate man. She shook her head, pushing away the silly notions. He was her patient, and he needed her full attention and care.

She walked back inside and concentrated on her duties. The last thing she wanted was for Head Nurse Valmont to get on her case and give her laundry duty as a punishment. More important, she didn't want to give the old hag something to use against her.

"Elodie, one of your patients is asking for you," Nurse Valmont said as Elodie entered the hall.

"Right away, madame." Elodie fixed her collar and straightened her sleeves before she walked into the quiet main room.

Around her, some patients slept while others read a book or talked with the doctor. She prayed all of them would return home instead of the front where more and more soldiers were killed or injured every day. She hoped this war would end soon so everyone could return to a somewhat normal life. But what life awaited her once the countries declared a ceasefire? She had no husband, no children, and her family had left Paris months ago. Where would she go? What would she do? Elodie took a deep breath and decided not to worry about the future for now. As she passed the patients, she wondered which one needed her. She had her share to care for and every one of them was sleeping peacefully—except one.

"You asked for me, Mr. Cassidy?"

He sat up with difficulty. Elodie helped him. "Gently, now," she said, holding him up and laying his back against the pillows.

"Thank you," he murmured.

His low baritone vibrated through her, causing a wave of heat within her depths. Before she lost herself in his intense gaze, she stepped back and gave him a smile. "Is there something you needed?"

"I wanted to know more about you. Where are you from?"

Elodie regarded him for a moment, unsure to share details of her life with a stranger. But she did learn over the months since she became a nurse that sharing a personal conversation with a patient could help with the healing process. "I am from Paris."

His tempting lips curled into a boyish grin. "Must have been nice growing up here."

"It is all right," she replied, sitting in the chair beside the bed. "Where are you from?"

"Texas."

"How nice!" That explained his accent she couldn't discern. "What brings you to France?"

"The Lafayette Escadrille. I'm a pilot."

"Isn't that dangerous?" She regretted her question. "Forgive me, but I've heard stories about how pilots die."

He shrugged a wide shoulder. "Only when we fight the enemy up there."

"Do you get scared?"

"No, I'm not afraid."

She stared at him, unbelieving he didn't get at least anxious when fighting the enemy in the air. Recalling what some French pilots had told her, anyone in their right mind would be terrified to face the enemy in a plane. If you were lucky, you could survive and fight another day. She shivered at the thought.

He leaned his head toward her and said, "I do pee my pants a bit, but don't tell anyone."

She giggled. "Do you remember anything about the crash?"

He glanced at his bandaged shoulder and said, "It's coming back to me." Jack squeezed his eyes, hissing at the pain.

She stood. "Are you all right? Do you need anything?"

He gently took her hand and gave her a reassuring smile. "Please stay. I'll be fine in a minute." He kept her fingers within his palm as she sat back in the chair. "Tell me more about you, Elodie."

"What you would like to know?"

"Do you have any brothers or sisters?"

She shook her head. "No, but I do have family in Provence."

"Where are your parents? Why aren't they here with you?"

Unshed tears stung her eyes. Sadness filled her. "They had to leave because food became scarce in the city."

"I'm so sorry to hear that. Who protects you here?"

She straightened her shoulders and said, "I can defend myself."

He smiled. "I'm sure you can."

Again, he studied her with his haunting blue eyes. Their surroundings faded with every racing heartbeat. His strong hand held onto hers, but this time she didn't pull away. She stared at his fingers twining with hers and mused at how they fit together with such perfection. Why did she feel as though she had known him all her life? She felt such an ease with Jack Cassidy. Maybe if they had met in a different time, they could have spent more time together, took walks in the park near the Eiffel Tower. With regret, she realized he was her patient—nothing more.

"I must return to my duties," she said, standing. "I will check on you later."

He gave a short nod and released her hand.

Elodie walked down the corridor and found a quiet corner. She lifted a hand against her lips to hide the smile forming on her face. Her heart raced so hard she thought she would faint from the excitement. What was happening to her? She didn't understand the wonderful feelings bubbling within her. Why couldn't she stop thinking of Jack Cassidy?

Chapter Two

Jack awoke feeling a searing pain in his shoulder.

He cursed under his breath, hoping the ache would go away. One smile from Elodie and all would be better. A grin curled on his lips at the thought. Glancing around the room, Jack wondered where she had gone. Come to think of it, he hadn't seen her this morning. Since the day they brought him in, she cared for him. Her presence reassured him. He didn't know her all that well, but there were times when he felt like he knew her all his life. How could that even be possible, he didn't know.

Screams from a young soldier jolted him out of his musings. Jack stilled in shock, seeing his body bandaged from head to toe. Since arriving in France, he hadn't seen what the war had done to all the men fighting in the trenches. As a pilot, he was fairly safe in his plane, except during combat. He'd witnessed some of his fellow pilots shot down only to collide with the ground. His best friend suffered this terrible fate at the hands of a German ace pilot.

Jack still had nightmares of that morning, images of his friend staring back at him in horror and shooting himself in the head before crashing. He preferred a quick death rather than burning and crashing. Jack squeezed his eyes, trying to block the pain of his loss incrusted in his heart. He promised himself not to make friends with any of the other pilots. He flew his plane into combat, did what he was told, and that was it.

Flashes of his own crashed plane resurfaced, almost chocking him. Bits and pieces returned every day. Now, he remembered all—even the face of the German bastard who shot him down. Jack shook his head, recalling how his gun jammed and how he tried escaping the enemy's shots. The German pilot saw he was in distress, but he shot at him anyway. He let out a low groan as anger rose within his gut. Jack couldn't wait to heal so he could return to his duties and find the coward who caused his crash and injuries. He hissed at the pain in his shoulder. *Dammit!*

"What are you doing?"

Jack looked up and saw Elodie with concern in her eyes. "I need to move a bit. Please," he pleaded with her, hoping she would agree to let him get some fresh air.

She put her hands on her slender hips and said, "Very well. Don't move. I'll get a wheelchair."

He let out a breath and smiled.

Elodie returned with a wheelchair and helped him get out of bed with ease. She put a blanket over his legs and thick socks on his feet. She lifted her chin and their eyes locked. He stared at her pretty face, making a mental picture for his cold, lonely nights. "Thank you," he said.

She didn't say a word, but gave him a smile that melted away the pain and frustration resounding in his body. He offered a hand for her to stand. She glanced at his fingers and laid hers within his palm. He wanted to hold her small hand forever. He wanted to hold her in his arms forever. She cleared her throat and rose.

"Let's get some fresh air," she said stepping behind him and pushing the chair out on the balcony.

"May we go for a walk around the grounds? I'd like to feel the sun on my face."

She hesitated for a moment, then pushed him down the ramp toward the stone path. Red and orange hues kissed the leaves on the trees around them. Peace and quiet surrounded him instead of the horrible screams. Soon, he would get away from this place. His heart sank. Once he recovered from his injuries, he would no longer see Elodie. He could no longer breathe. Taking a few deep breaths, he promised himself to visit her in Paris, if she accepted. He didn't know if she had a man in her life. He had never asked her. What a fool I am, he chided. He let his heart and raging desire for her overrule his head. Before he lost his mind and heart, he needed to know if she was free to love him. Now, was the best time to ask her.

"Do you have a loved one who is fighting in the war?" he asked, hoping not to sound too forward.

"No. Not anymore," she replied with sadness in her voice.

"What happened?"

She stopped the wheelchair. "My fiancé died."

"I'm sorry," he said with sincerity. "When did it happen?"

"A year ago."

Jack took her hand so she would face him. Without a moment of hesitation, he stood and wrapped his good arm around her. She was resistant to his touch at first, but then melted against his body, trembling. He drew her closer and held her tight. Her lavender perfume teased his nose. He closed his eyes, pretending for a moment she was his. A silly notion, he knew, but for now, it didn't matter.

* * * *

Elodie closed her eyes and let Jack hold her. She wanted to pull away, but his comforting arms made her forget her woes and the war raging around them. Why must he be so nice to her? He was her patient, nothing more could happen between them. Besides, once he left her care, she would never see him again.

"We should go back inside," she said stepping back.

Jack cupped her face and stared into her eyes. His thumb glided along her lips, coaxing them to open. A honeyed sensation pooled within her depths. Her breath slowed and her heart thumped with anticipation. Her gaze went to his tempting lips. If only she could taste him just once before she no longer saw him. He lifted her chin to kiss her cheek. His hot breath warmed her skin and radiated through her. His lips inched to the side and moved across hers in a slow tempting dance. Her head spun with a burning desire for Jack. *Heaven help me!* She was losing herself, her heart to this man she barely knew. She surrounded his neck with her arms, pulling him closer, feeling him. His tongue requested entrance and she let him in. No man had ever kissed her with such passion. A memory of her fiancé entered her mind. She broke Jack's spell before she lost herself to him forever. Stepping back, she touched her warm moist lips, oddly longing for another kiss.

"Please forgive me. I shouldn't have kissed you in such a manner," he replied with regret in his voice.

Elodie looked at him and saw the distress on his face. Her heart sank. She cleared her throat. "We should get back inside before they come looking for us."

While she helped Jack in the wheelchair, Elodie willed her heart to stop racing. She touched her lips, still feeling his mouth upon hers. She wished for more of his kisses, but it wasn't possible. A breath stuck in her throat as the thought of never seeing Jack again ran through her mind. Maybe if they had met in another time or place, love could be possible for them. She squeezed her eyes and chided herself for letting Jack kiss her and for letting herself feel again. She thanked the heavens no one saw them. Her cheeks warmed at the thought of them stealing a kiss. She couldn't recall one moment when her fiancé had done the same with her. No matter, she reasoned. Jack Cassidy will never kiss her again.

"Thank you for your kindness, mademoiselle," Jack said, gently grasping her hand.

"Do you need anything?" she asked, adjusting his pillow.

"I'd like some water, please."

Elodie poured him a glass and handed it to Jack. Their fingers touched, sending a spark through her arm. She bit her lower lip. The need to rest in Jack's arms grew with every moment passed in his presence. She wanted him to kiss her until she no longer felt her lips. She shook her head.

"Are you all right?" Jack's low baritone broke her reverie.

She gave a short nod.

"If you need to talk, I'm here," he said with honesty.

"I'll check up on you later." She smiled and released her hand slowly from his.

Elodie walked away, longing for some time alone. But her duties needed her attention first. The distraction, she hoped, would help her forget how much she wanted Jack's strong arms around her. She shook her head. "Stop thinking about Jack Cassidy," she chided herself. "He will only leave you too." Unshed tears stung her eyes as she folded clean linens. Before the head nurse saw her, Elodie wiped at her wet cheek and took a few deep breaths. Once Jack left the hospital, he would forget about her, and she would forget him.

She giggled. How could she forget him? He was unlike any other patient who came into her care. Something about him called out to her. His strength, courage and kindness toward her touched her to her very core. And his lips against hers made him unforgettable. She let out a low groan. Why must he be so irresistible?

A hand on her shoulder gave her a start. She lifted her head and saw Jack standing at the linen closet door. His wide shoulders filled the doorway. A breath caught in her throat.

"What are you doing here? If Nurse Valmont sees you here, she will have my hide."

He smiled. "I needed something."

She stood. "What is that?"

"This."

Jack caught her mouth with his, moving across her lips in a slow and delicious manner. His good arm drew her into his embrace. Her head spun, and she swore she saw stars behind her closed eyes. She searched for a hard surface with her hands and found his chest. A low moan escaped her throat when his tongue glided along her bottom lip. His mouth left hers and descended down her neck, gliding his tongue along the delicate spot behind her ear.

"Jack," she whispered.

"Hmm," he replied, feeling his hot breath against her ear.

Heat coursed through her blood, making her weak in the knees. She held on to Jack a bit more, wrapping her arms around his neck. "Kiss me."

His lips turned up in a boyish grin. "Say it again."

"Kiss me."

He granted her wish, tasting her lips once more. She lost herself in his embrace, wishing this moment never ended. Their bodies pressed against each other, she felt his growing desire for her. Or was it her imagination? His ragged breathing teasing her neck told her he wanted her as much as she desired him. She cupped his face and captured his lips as he had done to her. If they had no other moment like this, she wanted Jack to know how much she wanted him, how much he touched her heart in the short time they had known each other. As their tongues mingled, she tasted him until her mind blurred, no longer concerned with her surroundings. All she wanted was to feel Jack and remember this moment forever.

A soft knock at the closed door made Elodie jerk. Panic filled her.

"Hurry. You must hide," she said, helping Jack hide behind the door before fixing her hair.

She pulled on the knob and relaxed. . "Anything wrong?" Elodie asked Isabelle, hoping her friend didn't notice her heated cheeks.

"Nurse Valmont needs you."

"I'll be right there." Elodie closed the door and leaned her head against the cool hard surface.

"Please forgive me for getting you in trouble," Jack spoke behind her.

Elodie turned and cupped his strong jaw between her trembling hands. "You should return to your bed before someone realizes you're gone, or *you* will be in trouble."

He chuckled.

She loved his laugh. Without thinking, she took his lips between hers, tasting him one last time. "Please, leave," she whispered, leaning her head against his chest.

Jack lifted her chin. "I'll see you later."

She nodded.

He left her breathless once more. She let out a low groan, hoping the frustration building within her would leave. Why couldn't she resist Jack Cassidy? His touch and kisses left a lasting memory within her, and no matter how much she tried, she couldn't help wanting more of him. Taking a deep breath, she prayed for strength and for her heart to resist the only man who showed her passion. Was it already too late?

* * * *

Jack slid back into his bed without any of the nurses noticing he had gone.

He breathed a sigh of relief and closed his eyes, remembering Elodie's lips against his and her soft form melding to him. His body awoke with a desire he felt in every nerve. His blood coursed through him descending down his groin. If only they'd had a longer moment alone.

Something told him no other man held her heart. No woman kissed the way she did if she loved another man. He smiled. Excitement made his heart race a bit harder. He prayed they would have some time alone soon so he could touch her and hold her again. He wanted to know everything about her. For the first time in his life, a true chance at love and happiness called him. And he wanted to take this chance and see where it led him.

A shout from the bed beside him brought him back to reality. Jack looked around, but no nurse came to the soldier's aid. After a moment of hesitation, he got out of bed and went to help the young man. "Calm yourself," Jack said.

The young man looked at him with fear and confusion in his eyes. Bandages covered half his face. Jack felt sorry for him. "You're safe here. The doctors and nurses will fix you up real good. What's your name, soldier?"

"Eugene, monsieur," he replied with a thick French accent.

"Pleased to meet you, Eugene. My name is Jack Cassidy. Where are you from?"

"Normandy."

"I've visited once. Nice place."

"Yes, sir. That it is. Where are you from?"

"Texas."

"A cowboy, are you?" He chuckled.

Jack nodded. "Guilty."

"Have you been here long, sir?"

"A week. They take real good care of you here. Don't you worry."

"I want to go home."

A breath caught in Jack's throat. The soldier couldn't be more than twenty gauging by the thin stubble on his chin. *Poor kid, so far away from home to fight a war for his country.* "I'm sure you'll be home soon."

"Is everything all right here?" the familiar soft tone inquired.

Her lavender scent reached his nose. Again, Jack found himself imagining a time where no war existed, and Elodie was his to love and care for. If only he could take her in his arms at this moment. He ached for her touch. He shook his head, remembering where he was. Jack stood. "Eugene had a bad dream."

She smiled at him. Their eyes locked. "Thank you for caring. Now you get back in bed as well."

"Yes, mademoiselle," Jack said, holding back a chuckle.

Elodie tucked in Eugene, making sure he was comfortable. Then she helped Jack get under the covers. "Stay with me a bit," he asked, hoping she'd said yes.

She nodded. "Only a moment."

Jack stared at Elodie until his heavy eyelids closed from exhaustion. He held on to her small hand, as he dreamed of her. There, he pretended they lived a life together filled with love and children. He smiled.

"Why are you smiling?" she asked.

He opened his eyes and saw her lips had curled upward. "Nothing much."

"Something must have made you happy. Or someone?"

He chuckled. "Curious, are you?"

Elodie turned her head away. Jack leaned forward and tilted her chin so she looked at him. The need to taste her lips once more grew within him almost driving him mad. In her eyes, he swore he saw a hint of sadness and something else. He smiled, loving the notion she might be jealous of another woman who didn't exist. Leaning his head back against the pillow, he closed his eyes again.

"Tell me why are you smiling?"

"No reason. Just happy."

She stood. "I'll leave you to your dreams."

"No, please stay just a few minutes more. Until I fall asleep."

"All right. Another few minutes."

Jack closed his eyes and rested, dreaming of Elodie. He wished the war was over and he didn't have to return to his duties once he recovered from his injuries. *Dammit!* Maybe he should leave the Lafayette Escadrille so he could be free to do what he wanted? No. His parents had brought him up to respect his duties and keep his word. Besides, Elodie would never let him stay for her. She would want him to fight for her country.

He brought her fingers against his mouth and pressed his lips inside her palm. He wanted to tell her how much she meant to him despite the short time they have known each other, but the words stuck in his throat. She would think he was crazy for sure if he told her how much his heart sang whenever she was around. For now, he reasoned, he would spend every moment he could with the woman who had stolen his heart.

Chapter Three

Elodie chewed on her lower lip until she tasted blood.

Maybe she should have told Jack in person about the Nurse Valmont's decision to send her to one of the hospitals on the front. In the weeks since Jack had arrived in her care, they had spent hours together. They had become each other's confidents. She would miss their daily walks in the hospital gardens. As a tear rolled down her cheek, she wiped it away before her friend Henri noticed. The last thing she wanted was for him to see her weak.

"We'll arrive soon," Henri announced.

Glancing at the golden French fields from the truck window, Elodie's heart sank. Her country had been violated by the enemy. She prayed the Huns would never reach Paris. Thanks to brave men like Jack, they would defend France with their own blood. She held back a smile thinking of Jack. Her heart called out his name. If only she had one more moment with him, alone. She closed her eyes and imagined his strong arms holding her, protecting her. She shook her head, knowing Jack would never come for her. She had lost her last chance at love.

"Do not worry, *ma belle*. You will see your *amoureux* again soon."

Elodie stared at her friend and wondered why he would say such a thing. "Excuse me?"

"You are sad because you have left behind the man you love."

Words stuck in her throat. She had never realized before this moment the possibility of loving Jack. Did he love her too? She went over all the time she spent with him. He never mentioned the words of love. They kissed and held hands, but only in secret. Maybe he didn't love her at all. Maybe he was lonely and only wanted her companionship until he healed and left the hospital. What a fool I've been, she chided herself. She let Jack Cassidy kiss her and touch her without any intention of loving her. She didn't leave behind the man she loved. She left a soldier in need of physical contact, that's it.

"Do not worry, you will see him again."

"I don't think so, Henri. He is not my lover."

He chuckled. "I have known you long enough to see when you are in love."

"How can you tell?"

"The smile on your face. You never had such a smile. And your eyes sparkle when you think of him."

Elodie stared out the truck window again and felt her heart sink a bit more. "He does not love me."

"Maybe he does, but you do not see it."

For the rest of the drive, Elodie forced herself again to remember if her fiancé ever loved her. He treated her with respect and cared for her, and he did love her. But he never showed her the same passion Jack had in the few weeks they spent together. Why hadn't she noticed before now? Was this what Henri meant? She turned to her friend and asked, "What happens now? I will never see Jack again."

"You will. Love always finds a way."

She hoped Henri was right. Despair gnawed at her. She had no way to return to Paris. She couldn't leave her duties at the frontline hospital no matter how much she wanted to. With all her strength, she pushed back the growing need to ask Henri to stop the truck so she could go back to Paris and find Jack. Maybe if she wrote him a letter, letting him know how much she wanted to be with him and loved him. The idea made her smile. The doctor would release him at the end of the week, so she had some time to write him. He'd receive her letter before he left the hospital.

* * * *

Jack took one last look around, hoping Elodie would walk into the room before he left.

He squeezed his eyes, pushing away the hurt and disappointment raging within his gut. He felt like such a fool for opening his heart to Elodie. *Maybe I scared her away*, he thought with regret. *Dammit!* Now, he'd never be able to tell her how much he loved her. If only he could see her one last time before he returned to the war he hated. It had brought him to Elodie, but had also taken her away from him. When he read her note this morning saying she was leaving for the front, he knew at that moment he wanted to spend the rest of his life with her. He wanted to wake with her every morning and sleep with her every night. Now that may never happen because of this bloody war. He had no idea where to find her or where to start looking.

"Your ride is here, Monsieur Cassidy."

Jack turned and nodded. Inhaling a deep breath, he grabbed his canvas bag and followed the head nurse down the long corridor. Outside, a truck waited for him. He lifted his head and glanced heavenward. The cloudy sky reflected his mood. A long ride toward the front awaited him. He prayed in silence for one more chance to see Elodie so he could hold her in his arms and whisper in her ear the love he felt for her.

"Let's go," he told the driver as he closed the truck door.

Jack leaned his head back and closed his eyes, hoping the ride toward the front would be short. But he knew the trip could take hours before they reached their destination. He had his orders and his commanding officer waited for him near the town of Reims. His shoulder had completely healed, so Thénault would expect him to continue his duties. *Anything to finish this war so he could be reunited with Elodie.*

As they drove through the countryside, Jack imagined building his own house here one day. He loved France since the first moment his feet hit the ground. He had seen the country from the earth and the air, and he loved every part. A smile curled his lips when images of a life with Elodie formed in his tired head. Excitement made his heart flutter. He needed to find her. But he wondered where to start? She could be anywhere in France. The head nurse wouldn't tell him where she had gone.

"I'm sorry, monsieur. That information is confidential," she told him earlier this morning.

The old hag didn't want to budge one inch no matter how much coaxing. He even promised her a box of chocolates, but she refused with a giggle. Someone had to know where the hospital had sent her. But who? Maybe Thénault would know.

"Can you go any faster," Jack asked the driver gently.

He shook his head. "Sorry. This old truck is going as fast as possible."

Jack let out a low groan and rubbed his hands across his face. He could only close his eyes and rest, hoping they'd reach their destination soon. For now, he concentrated on seeing Elodie. The image of her sweet face popped in his head. He recalled every moment spent with her. When he came to France all those months ago, he never imagined falling in love. Her beauty inside and out touched him to his very core. She made him tremble with anticipation and need. He loved Elodie, and wanted to tell her as soon as he found her.

"Ah! Le coup de foudre!"

Jack looked at the driver and smiled. "Is it that obvious Cupid hit me in the behind with a bolt of lightning?"

"I would say so. Who is she?"

"Elodie."

"Elodie Paradis?" he asked, surprised.

"Yes. You know her?"

The driver nodded. "Of course. She is my friend. I drove her to Reims the other day."

A breath caught in Jack's throat. He finally knew where they had sent Elodie. And he was going to see her soon. His heart raced with anticipation and excitement. His prayer was answered. In only a few short hours, he would hold her in his arms and declare his love to her. He hoped she wanted him too.

"Did she say anything about me?"

The man chuckled. "The poor girl is in love with you too. But do not tell her I said so."

"I promise." Jack could barely contain his excitement. "Have you known her a long time?" he asked, curious.

"Elodie is like my daughter. She lives with my wife and me at our house. Her parents are our friends. When they had to leave Paris, they asked us to care for her. She has lost her fiancé in the war, and a lot of her close friends have also died. The damn Germans killed them while they were traveling to a safer place."

Jack felt his heart break. "She told me about her parents leaving, but she never said anything about their death. I thought they were living with relatives in the country?"

"That is where they were headed with her brother. But the Germans had been raiding farm houses along the road to the country. Her parents thought it was safe and that the enemy hadn't reached the village."

"Why didn't she tell me?"

"Elodie is a very proud girl. She never wants to talk about her feelings or anything else. But I know her. When I saw the smile on her face, she couldn't hide from me the love she has for you."

"She loves me?"

"Very much, but she is afraid."

"Of what?"

"That you will leave her like her fiancé, like her family. She loved him, but with you it is not the same. There is a sparkle in her eyes I have never seen. Promise me you will care for her and love her with all your heart."

Jack nodded. "I promise."

* * * *

Elodie took a deep breath, but the stale air made her choke.

She missed home. Every day since she had arrived in Reims, she had seen more of her fair share of patients. Not one moment passed had she stayed idle, and that was all right with her. She didn't want to miss home or Jack. Unshed tears stung her tired eyes. Why couldn't she stop thinking of Jack? If only she could see him one last time before the war ended. She laughed at the idea. He was probably long gone by now, fighting the enemy in his plane. When she left the hospital, he had almost fully recovered from his injuries suffered a month before. She glanced at the sky as French fighter planes flew over her. The Lafayette Escadrille had their base nearby. Maybe Jack was there too, she hoped.

She rubbed her arms against the chilled late morning breeze and brought her mind to the present. Rubble from the bombed buildings surrounded her. Every day, men from town cleared up the streets for the ambulances and people who traveled toward the country. They fled for safety. She would do the same if the hospital no longer needed her. But she wanted to be in Reims to help the wounded and dying. It was her duty, and she didn't mind. Again, she thought of how she missed Jack and wanted to see him.

"Please God, let me see Jack one last time," she whispered in the breeze.

"I'm here, my darling."

She opened her eyes. "Jack."

He took a step closer and drew her in his arms. "My sweet Elodie."

"Am I dreaming?"

"No, love. You're not dreaming."

Elodie held Jack tight, never wanting to let him go. "Please don't leave me."

"I promise to keep you with me forever."

She looked into his eyes. "What about the war?"

"I will come back to you. You have my word."

"You can't do that," she said, pulling away. "What happens if the enemy shoots you down again?"

Jack wrapped his arms around her and murmured against her ear. "I'll be careful. Besides, I'm much safer up there than on the ground. And I'm a good shot."

"Aren't you afraid?"

He gently turned her. "Yes, but you give me strength. Your love protects me."

"When will I see you again?"

"Soon, my love. For now, I'm here with you. Thénault allowed me some time. We have a night together, if you want me."

She cupped his face between her shaky hands. "I'm yours, Jack." Uncaring who saw them, Elodie caught Jack's lips, letting him know how much she had missed him and loved him. "I love you, Jack Cassidy," she whispered.

"I love you too, Elodie Paradis."

"Come." She took his hand and led him inside to a quiet corner of the hospital.

Jack closed the door to the small room she had slept in since she arrived in Reims. He stared at her with his burning gaze. She bit her lower lip, feeling the heat flaming through her. "I want you, Jack."

He pulled her against him. "Say it again."

"I want you."

His lips found hers and moved across them, tempting. A low gasp escaped her throat when his tongue invited hers in a slow tango. His fingers tugged at the buttons of her gown and pushed the fabric down while his teeth grazed her shoulder. Desire made her head spin. She searched for a stable surface and anchored herself to his narrow waist. *Heaven help me!* She wanted Jack more than she needed air. She removed his tie and unbuttoned his shirt, finding a soft white cotton undershirt. Her fingers found their way under the fabric and touched his hot skin. He let out a low groan.

"Did I hurt you?"

He shook his head. "No, love. Your touch pleases me."

Encouraged, she let her hands roam over the flat planes of his stomach, reveling in the texture of his skin. Soft yet thick. She lifted the undershirt to kiss his skin, smiling when he groaned again. Resting her head against his chest, she listened to his racing heart beat. His hand caressed her hair and cheek while he kissed the top of her head.

She lifted her chin and looked into his eyes. "Kiss me."

He smiled and pressed his lips to hers again, tasting her. Then he lifted her off the floor and laid her on the bed. He stared at her for a moment. "I love you, Elodie. Know that I will be yours forever."

Tears flooded her eyes. "I love you too, Jack. I will wait for you."

A tear rolled down his cheek while his fingers ran over her face as if he had no sight. Her heart squeezed, as she wiped the tear away from his face. "We'll be together soon, *mon amour*."

He nodded and kissed her, sealing their promise to each other.

The End

SWEET LOVE REMEMBERED
Jean C. Joachim
Copyright © 2012

"Get out of the car."

"What'd I say?"

"Get out." Perri shifted the car into drive.

"Look, Perri, the kid's been gone for five years already. When are you gonna let go?" Ike closed the door but leaned on the open window, in no hurry to leave.

"Mike. The kid's name was Mike," Perri said as she peeled out, depressing the gas pedal almost to the floor. "Asshole."

Perri slowed down when she crossed the George Washington Bridge into New Jersey. She forked right onto the Palisades Parkway, then leaned back against the rich leather seat of her BMW. The drive to Pine Grove was so familiar she could do it in her sleep.

You'd be five today, Mikey. If you had lived. It's five years since we scattered your ashes in Cedar Lake.

June twenty-second, the day before Mikey's birthday, was the day of Perri's annual trip to Pine Grove. She took a shaky breath. SIDS took four-month-old Michael Jessup. The son of Perri and Sergeant Matthew Jessup…once her husband, now her ex.

Perri pulled into the driveway of the Pine Grove Guesthouse facing Cedar Lake. She had a standing reservation for the same week every year. Lacy Ryan, gray-haired owner of the guesthouse, had Perri's room ready. She took a freshly baked cookie off the plate Lacy was holding.

"Room's ready, Perri." Lacy hugged the pretty brunette.

"What's all that lumber in old Doc Branford's yard?" Perri munched on her cookie.

"Doc moved to Florida. Somebody bought the place. Fixin' it up too." Lacy took the plate into the kitchen. "Coffee's still hot."

Perri felt a twinge in her gut. Doc Branford's house was the house she and Matt stayed in on their brief honeymoon. He was on leave from the Marines when they met. Every year Perri peered at the old place from next door, watching it get more dilapidated and seedy. She couldn't bear to stay there. Too many memories...it's where Mike was conceived. They stayed there again when they brought his ashes up...when they had that brutal fight. Perri shook her head to get rid of the memory.

"He wouldn't have died if you'd been here instead of Afghanistan!" she screamed at him.

"You...you let my son die!" he hollered back.

The shouting match echoed in her brain as if she was hearing it for the first time. Her stomach knotted as the horrible words they exchanged knifed through her gut.

"You all right? Ya look kinda pale," Lacy asked. She put her hand on Perri's forearm as she guided her into the kitchen.

"Do you know who bought Doc's place?" Perri took a sip of her coffee.

"Nope. Haven't seen him yet." Lacy fumbled with her cup, nearly dropping it.

"Think I'll take a look after I unpack."

"Oh, I wouldn't do that. Trespassing. It's somebody's property...he probably don't like people snooping around."

Perri shot Lacy a quizzical look, but the older woman avoided her glance.

* * * *

Perri threw her clothes in the drawers of the small dresser in her tidy room. She slung her camera case over her shoulder, donned her sunglasses, then descended the stairs. *Still time for a couple of good shots of the lake or Lacy's flower garden.* Once outside, curiosity got the best of her so she approached Doc's property cautiously. There was a car in the driveway. Some of the lumber was gone. She stepped over the short hedge separating Lacy's place from Doc's, then tiptoed toward the front window. The curtain was open. She leaned forward, peering in, shading her eyes with her hands.

Familiar strains of the *1812 Overture* met her ears over the sporadic whirr of an electric drill. She spied the naked back of a tall man, wearing jeans. His shoulders seemed to stretch from one wall of the living room to the other. In the middle of his back was a

The Call of Duty

small tattoo. She bolted upright, pulling away from the window. *How many men have a tattoo of a periwinkle flower! Matt!*

He'd gotten it one night in the service as a reminder of her. Chills went through her. *Matt's here? What for? He bought this place? Why?* After their horrendous fight, Matt stormed out. He moved out the next day. She filed for divorce and hadn't seen him since. *Lacy knew!* Perri set her mouth in a thin line. Lacy knew about Matt. *Why should I care? I don't even use his last name anymore.* Her colleagues in the advertising world knew her as Perri Lochner, not Perri Jessup.

The sound of the drill stopped. *Oh my God. I don't want him to see me, like a peeping tom!* She panicked, moved too quickly, and caught her foot on a root. She went down with a thud mixed with a cry of pain as her ankle twisted. The front door swung open, and there he stood, staring down at her.

"Perri? Is that you?"

She nodded, training her gaze on her ankle, afraid to look him in the eye.

"What are you doing here?" he asked, approaching her while extending his hand.

Perri was mortified but grabbed his hand anyway, needing help to get to her feet. A tingle shot up her arm at the contact with his skin. His touch was warm and dry, like always.

"Are you all right?" he asked.

Perri bent over and rubbed her ankle. When she saw his gaze zero in on the neckline of her tank top, she realized she was putting on a pretty good show. She righted herself, annoyed at the amused look on his face.

"I might ask you the same question," she said, stiffly.

"I got leave for Mike's fifth birthday," he said it bluntly without further explanation.

He's the only one who calls him Mike besides me.

"Me too."

"Leave? You joined the military?"

"No, no. I'm working in advertising now. I always take this week as vacation."

"So you come up here every year?"

She nodded.

"You're lucky. This is the first time I've been able to get here on his birthday. Usually I have to come on some unimportant day. So your company gives you a couple of days for this?"

"They don't know where I go."

"Oh? Why not?" He rested his hands on his hips.

"They're not big on women with kids...and though I'm not exactly a woman with a kid...I...well—"

"I get it." He cut her off, saving her further embarrassment.

"You've been coming here?" As she glanced up, her eyes connected with his.

"Haven't missed a year since..." His voice trailed off but Perri heard the clutch of emotion in his tone, making her want to touch him. She stepped back instead, studying his face.

The tragedy had left its mark. Grief had etched fine lines around his eyes and mouth but the rest remained untouched. The lines added character. His eyes were still the brightest blue, the same eyes as Mikey. His brown hair worn very short hadn't grayed since the loss. *God, he's still so handsome.* Something inside her fluttered.

"Me, neither," she piped up to cover his discomfort.

"What do you do to celebrate?"

"Nothing. I don't have a birthday cake like some whack job. I realize he's...gone. Might sit on the dock or row out to the middle of the lake...think about what he'd have been like. Nothing special."

"I never said you were a whack job..." His voice became tense.

"Please don't start, Matt. We've been so civilized..." Perri put up a hand.

"Haven't we?" He raised an eyebrow.

"Are you married?" The question popped out of her mouth before she could stop it.

"No. You?"

She shook her head.

"Dating anyone?" he asked.

"Was...until he referred to Mikey as *the kid*. We weren't dating long. It doesn't matter." She waved her hand.

"His loss. You look good." His gaze traveled her length, focusing in the usual places.

A smile crinkled the lines around his eyes. The warmth emanating from his stare sent a shiver rocketing up her spine. *One look from him…I'm putty. Still.*

"Thanks. You're still in the Marines?"

"Yup. It's my life."

"No woman?"

"No one special."

She nodded her head like she understood but she didn't understand at all why some woman hadn't snatched him up years ago.

"I was almost engaged…but she wanted kids and I…" He wiped his hands on his jeans.

"I know. Seems as if all guys want to have kids. Been there."

His smile became grim.

"I get it."

"Knew you would." A small smile crossed her lips. She stared at him as a hunger grew inside her. *I wonder if he tastes the same.* She stole a glance at his lips.

"Want to come in for coffee?" He stepped aside, gesturing to the front door.

"I've got to get back…unpack," she lied, brushing leaves off her butt.

He nodded.

"Surprised you haven't done that yet, you're always so efficient."

"Yeah. That's me…except when it came to keeping our son alive."

Matt closed his fingers over her forearm.

"It wasn't your fault." She saw something in his expression, something she didn't expect…understanding.

"Funny you feel that way now. You didn't then." Perri looked up directly into his eyes, challenging him.

"Please don't, Perri. Let's not revisit that…that…terrible night."

She stepped back.

"You're right."

"Perri, I…about that night…I'm…"

She raised her hand to stop him.

"Water under the bridge, Matt. Gotta go. Nice to see you."

She turned on her heel to make a fast getaway. When she got to Lacy's door, she glanced back at him. His head hung low, his hand covered his eyes. Her throat closed up, emotion choking her. Her palm flattened against the door, her arm jutted out straight supporting her weight. Tears clouded her eyes. After several deep breaths, she opened the door and disappeared inside.

By ten o'clock, Perri lay exhausted but restless, unable to sleep. Tangled up in the sheet, she rolled over to peek through the open window to Matt's house. There was a light on in the upstairs bedroom. He didn't bother to draw the curtains. *Not a modest bone in his body. That hasn't changed.* She smiled at the memory of the first time he dropped his clothes. He dove in the lake stark naked in front of her, then urged her to join him.

Perri pushed up on her elbow to watch him get ready for bed. He stripped down to his boxers. Her pulse kicked up as her gaze followed the outline of his hard body. Her fingertips twitched, wanting to touch his smooth skin, brush through the hair on his chest. He walked over to the dresser, picked up a picture and kissed it. Then he dropped his boxers, pulled down the covers and got into bed. She wondered if it was a picture of Mikey he kissed or one of her with Mikey. *Probably just Mikey.*

Perri moistened her lips with her tongue, her mouth suddenly dry at the sight of Matt's naked body. The memory of what he used to do to her with his wonderful body flooded her mind, causing heat long dormant to flow in her veins again. She ached to feel his touch. *Stop it! Remember what he said to you. How angry, how vitriolic…his accusations.*

When Matt switched out his light, Perri rolled over on her back. She could almost feel his skin, his body resting lightly on hers. *It's been such a long time. I've got to let him go.* Tension in her neck relaxed. Perri felt drowsy, nodding off to sleep.

* * * *

Perri slept in the morning of Mikey's birthday. She awoke at nine to a beautiful late June day. The sun was shining. *Was it shining the morning he was born? I can't remember.*

A feeling of panic grabbed her chest. *Am I forgetting? Details, things I used to think about all the time…am I forgetting Mikey?*

The Call of Duty

For a moment, she couldn't breathe. She slumped down on the front stoop of Lacy's house, putting her head in her hands. Then it came to her. *Yes! It was sunny all day. After my water broke, it clouded up. I had to take my sunglasses off to drive to the hospital.* Her breathing returned to normal. She had driven herself to the hospital because Matt had been in Afghanistan. He arrived two days after Mikey was born.

Perri looked up when she heard the front door of Matt's house open. There he stood in T-shirt and jeans, filling the doorway. A worried expression on his face caught her attention. He walked over to Lacy's.

"Are you all right?" he asked, standing a respectful distance from her.

She nodded.

"Temporary memory loss."

"I'll bet you remember every detail of Mikey's birth, his life..."

"I should. I've been reliving it in my mind for five years."

"Would you mind reliving his birth one more time...for me? Since I wasn't there...what you told me...faded. I want to remember that too." His voice was even, careful not to stir any anger or hostility.

"You didn't have much time with him, did you?" For a moment, sympathy crowded out resentment in her heart. *You missed his first smile, his first walk outside.*

"Not as much as you. But I thought about him every day. I had his picture with me all the time...it's what kept me safe. I felt connected to him even though we were so far apart. So, would you mind?"

"Okay." He joined her on the stoop.

"It started out a sunny day, just like this one..."

They sat for half an hour while Matt listened intently as Perri spun the story of Mikey's birth one more time. Her mouth softened into a smile as she reminisced. His eyes never left her face.

"When they handed him to me, I cried." She paused to take a deep breath. "It hurt so much you weren't there..." Her eyes got misty.

"You knew what I did for a living when you married me," Matt spoke softly.

"We hardly knew each other at all. We got married because you were sure you'd knocked me up." Perri jerked to attention, her eyes hooded.

"That is a joke. Were you really too dense to get it? My excuse for getting you to marry me." There was an edge to his voice.

"Really? An excuse? What happened to love and romance?" Perri cocked an eyebrow.

"It's hard to romance someone as prickly as you." Matt leaned away from her.

"I'm prickly? We jumped into an affair, then a marriage so fast because of your stupid job. Hey, pardon me for missing my husband at the birth of my child." Perri stood up.

"Stupid job? Being a Marine is an honor, a privilege, a responsibility."

"What about your responsibility to me?" Perri wanted to take the sharpness out of her voice, wanted to stop baiting him but couldn't.

"I tried Perri." Matt pushed to his feet.

"Yeah? Did you? Well that doesn't cut it. Not then or now, either."

Matt grabbed her arm as she turned to go.

"Why are we fighting? It was five years ago." His grip tightened.

She faced him. "Seems to be what we do best."

"Mikey was what we did best." Matt's voice softened.

Tears stung the back of Perri's eyes. She covered her mouth with her hand.

"You're right…he's what we did best," she muttered.

Silence fell on them like a blanket of fog.

"I'm here now, Perri. Let's share this," he pleaded with her.

"I'm afraid." Her voice was barely audible.

"I know. Me too." He slipped his arm around her shoulders.

"I've got stuff to do…call in to work…" Perri eased away from Matt.

"Sure, sure." Matt backed off. "I've got work to do in the house."

She jumped in her car, then raced out the driveway. *Need to get away.* She drove aimlessly ending up on the banks of the Delaware River at their special spot. This was where they had their most memorable date—a canoe trip to shoot the rapids. Matt fell in the river at the end. He picked her up and threw her in too. It was September, there was a chill in the air. Matt brought her back to his grandparent's house where he built a fire. His grandparents had gone on vacation leaving Matt in charge of the house for a week during his two month leave from the Marines. Perri and Matt stripped down, then hung their clothes to dry. Lying in front of the fire, wrapped in a blanket, they made love for the first time. She remembered every touch, every cry as well as she remembered Mike's birth.

Perri drove slowly by his grandparent's house. New owners repainted it. The tired beige was now barn red. Two young children played in the front yard while their mother weeded the garden.

Perri had fallen in love with that old farmhouse. Matt could have had it too. In fact they thought about buying the place once they got married. But Perri returned to her teaching job in the city when Matt returned to Afghanistan. After they lost Mikey, all their other plans fell apart. She felt a sharp pain in her chest looking at the happy house. *We would've been a family too.*

Perri spent the day visiting the places she had frequented with Matt—the little hole-in-the-wall restaurant with great chicken fingers and hot fudge sundaes, then the quirky gift shop in Oak Bend. She went to Homer's for dinner, selecting a table facing Cedar Lake. Her mind wandered back to happy days with Matt, eating in the same spot—at the same table, in fact.

"This seat taken?"

A deep, warm voice jarred Perri from her reverie. She turned to face Matt. His face looked so apologetic, almost pathetic. *How can I turn him away?*

"Sit." She pushed the chair toward him.

He angled the chair to face the lake.

"Where'd you go?" He pulled up to the table.

"Huh?"

"You disappeared after our talk." His fingers toyed with hers but didn't take them in his warm grasp.

"I drove around. Visited a few old favorite places. Saw Dry Gorge Ranch."

"My grandparents sold it to a young couple. By now they've probably got a couple of kids."

"Plus a dog. They painted the house red."

"Red? I'd thought about cream...tan...never red."

Perri laughed. "Yeah, me too."

They ordered bacon cheeseburgers and beer, then ate in silence.

"How's the house coming?" she asked him before finishing the last of her beer.

"Needs a lot of work. The place was a dump when we stayed there. After five years of neglect...it's a shame."

"What a place for a honeymoon." She laughed.

"You didn't seem to mind." His stare got warm again, a knowing smile on his lips.

"I had other things on my mind." She shot him a sexy grin.

"You sure did." His gaze dropped to her breasts for a moment.

"I wasn't exactly alone in those thoughts, if I recall."

"No you weren't," he snickered. "You were amazing."

"So were you." She felt a stirring in her loins, remembering what an excellent lover Matt had been. She hadn't experienced anything like his lovemaking since.

The waitress came to clear the table.

"Can I get you something else?"

"Do you still have the best cheesecake in the county?" Matt asked.

"Annabelle's cheesecake? You bet we do."

Matt glanced over at Perri, raising his eyebrows in an unspoken question.

"I'm done." She shook her head.

"Share a piece?" Matt reached over, resting his hand close to Perri's.

"Really, I shouldn't." She left her hand near his.

"It's only half." He brushed his hand against hers, then gave it a little squeeze before he shifted in his seat, removing his hands from the table.

"Okay." She felt his touch like the sear of a flame.

"One piece of Annabelle's with two forks. Coming up." The waitress picked up the heavy tray and carted it away.

"Probably not as good as the sundaes at Cone Shanty, though. I went there yesterday. God, their hot fudge sauce…and it's still great."

"I know! I've been looking all over Manhattan for good hot fudge. It must be homemade."

"Everything was sweeter when I shared it with you." Matt's hand crept closer, the tips of his fingers brushed against hers.

A small smile curled Perri's lips. *We shared a large hot fudge sundae because it was cheaper than two smalls. Licking the fudge off his lips.* A flush of heat spread through her chest at the memory.

The cheesecake arrived. He held the first forkful up to Perri's lips. She opened her mouth, locking her gaze on his. Matt's gaze followed her tongue as it slid the luscious confection off the fork, swallowed, then licked her lips. He looked deep into her mahogany eyes. Desire flickered there for a moment. Perri reached out to touch his rough cheek with her forefinger. He flinched, causing her to snatch her hand away.

"Sorry. I'm not used to…being touched…especially by you."

"No problem. Won't do it again." She leaned back, veiling her expression, fighting to keep the choke of emotion out of her voice.

He grimaced.

"I did it again. I should have *I'm sorry* tattooed on my forehead." His gaze dropped to his hands as he fiddled with a napkin.

"I get to use Lacy's old rowboat. It's part of my deal. I'm rowing out to the center of the lake for a while tonight. Do you wanna come?"

"Would I be intruding on your privacy?" He crossed his legs.

"I asked you, didn't I?"

"Ah, always the lady…"

She detected sarcasm in his voice. "Ouch! Hey, don't come. Not like I care whether or not." She wiped the corners of her mouth with her napkin.

"Okay, okay. I'll come." He put both feet on the ground.

"I don't give a sh—"

"*I'm coming!*" He bolted upright.

People at other tables glanced nervously at Matt and Perri.

"Thanks for the invite," he said so quietly it was almost a whisper.

"You're welcome." She shifted in her chair.

The check arrived. Perri reached for it but Matt whisked it away before she could.

"I'm paying." Matt set his chin firmly.

"Look. I make a good salary. I can afford to pay my half."

"Nope. I'm paying. Least I can do after…"

"Please, forget it." She waved her hand.

"I'm paying." He spoke quietly but firmly.

"Okay, okay. You wanna pay, go right ahead!"

"Why can't you make anything easy?" He slammed his credit card down on the table.

* * * *

It was a comfortably cool, clear night, typical of June in Pine Grove. Matt and Perri met at the dock. She stepped gingerly into the small rowboat. Matt untied the rope, then boarded. Watching him man the oars, Perri noted how at ease he was on the water. She relaxed. Being with him on Cedar Lake again seemed natural to her.

"What direction?"

Perri pointed toward the middle of the lake. The full moon lit their way, making the journey easier.

"Here." He paused to hand her a small flashlight.

"There's enough moonlight."

"You never know."

"Always prepared, always the Marine, aren't you?"

He snickered. "I wasn't the last time we made love. You didn't object."

"How gallant of you to remind me," she quipped.

"Please. Can we stop bickering…just for tonight." He halted the oars to stare into her brown eyes.

"In Mikey's honor. I'll behave."

Matt blew out a breath before he continued rowing. Under the steady movement of Matt's arms, they reached the center of the lake quickly. Perri watched his muscles work, causing the boat to glide noiselessly through the water. In his wifebeater shirt she got a good view of his arms, including part of his broad chest. Her eyes drank greedily of the sight soon to be gone…forever. He raised the oars, balancing them on the sides of the boat. The only sound was the gentle lapping of small waves against the wood. Perri glanced at the moon, then at Matt. The moon shone on his hair, shadowed half his face, while kissing the other half with a warm glow. *God, he's gorgeous.*

She wanted to fall into his arms. This had been one of her dreams, sharing Mikey's birthday with Matt. She thought it'd never happen. She craved the comfort of his arms, to share the memory, but the gap between them seemed as wide as the Delaware River.

* * * *

Matt didn't know what to expect when he met Perri at the boat. He took control. *Keep busy. Don't think. Row.* In his usual way, he did what he could to make her feel safe, taking the oars, moving the boat through the water while she sat back, watching. *Her sorrow has added to her beauty.* He watched the moon shine off her dark hair. Though her eyes were shadowed, he felt her gaze on him. The electricity, the chemistry they once had, returned. His palms began to sweat so he rubbed them on his jeans. *Can't row with sweaty hands.* She shifted in her seat. He noticed the slight jiggle of her breasts. His hands ached to touch her. The moonlight made the swell of her breasts above the low neckline of her tank top too inviting. He couldn't shift his gaze.

Memories of making love to Perri flashed through his mind. The softness of her skin, the firmness of her flesh, her sweet scent, how it felt to be inside her, coupled with her passion for him made him feel growing pressure between his legs. *Control yourself! This is about Mikey.* He forced his gaze to return to the dock, glancing at the dark houses hugging the lake. *Mikey would've loved it here.* Suddenly another image pushed out his sexy memories. Visions of a five-year-old boy with dark hair and bright blue eyes sitting on the dock fishing with his father tore his heart. The image of something never to be made his eyes water. He put the oars up on the sides of the boat to let it drift for a bit. A deep sigh slipped from his lips.

"You okay?" Her voice sounded softer than before.

He nodded as emotion had stolen his words.

Before he knew it, Perri leaned forward to take his hand. She squeezed his palm between hers, then laced her fingers with his.

"It's harder than you expect." Her gaze sought his.

"He'd be five," he choked out.

She lowered her head. He saw something shine in the moonlight...tears on her cheek. Cupping his big hands under her armpits, he yanked her up off her seat, pulling her into his arms. After sliding Perri onto his lap, he wound his arms around her. The boat teetered a bit making the water slosh gently against the sides, then settle down. His thumb traced her tears, wiping them away. Neither spoke. Matt held her tight, resting his chin on her head. Perri curled into his embrace with a sigh, hiding her face in his chest. *God, I miss holding her...the scent of her hair.* He leaned down toward her neck. *Her skin...wonderful.* He took a deep breath, closing his eyes. *I never thought this would happen again.*

"Happy birthday, Mikey. I...we miss you," Matt whispered.

Perri snaked her arms around his middle to stroke his back. For a minute, Matt could swear they were still married, clinging to each other for support, the way they should have. The warmth of her embrace calmed him. He relaxed, his body swaying slightly this way and that with the movement of the boat.

"How long is your leave?" Perri's shaky voice broke the silence.

"Only five more days." He stroked her hair.

"Me too."

I have to make the most of this time with her. We need peace.

About midnight, Perri let go of Matt. Placing her hands on his chest, she pushed a little attempting to stand up. *Feels so good...her hands on me again.* Matt placed his hand under her elbow, helping her to rise.

"Thanks." She returned to her side of the boat, wrapping her arms around her middle. "It's late."

"Aye, aye, Captain. Heading for shore," Matt said as he picked up each oar.

Perri turned to look at the moonlight shining on the center of the lake one last time. She let out a deep breath.

"Bye, Mikey. See you next year." She blew a kiss before she turned to face the dock.

* * * *

The next morning, the doorbell at Lacy's rang repeatedly until Perri padded downstairs in her bathrobe to answer it. The deliveryman handed her a bouquet of apricot roses with a letter attached. She took a whiff of her favorite flowers, then thanked the man. Once inside, she put the flowers in water before pouring herself a cup of coffee. Excited but nervous, she ripped open the note.

> *You wouldn't let me say this in person, so I'm saying it here. I'm sorry, so terribly sorry for all the things I said to you that night. I was angry, hurt, devastated...so many hopes gone. I took it out on you. That wasn't fair.*
>
> *I didn't really believe what I said. I wanted to hurt someone because I was hurting. So I lashed out at you. I never thought you'd take it so seriously and divorce me. You don't know how many times I've regretted those words. I hope you can forgive me so we can move on without any more bad feelings. I wish you a happy life.*
> *Matt*

Perri sank down into a chair at the kitchen table. Here it was, the apology she'd been waiting five years to receive. But his desire to move on hurt almost as much as his angry words. He said he was sorry but he wanted to move on. She'd hoped to see *I still love you* in the note, *let's get back together*, something...something more. When he took her in his arms in the rowboat, Perri felt something inside her switch, change.

Much of the anger she felt at his desertion dissipated when he held her. She had needed Matt so much, needed to be in his arms after Mike died but he wasn't there. Now, five years later, the warmth of his embrace soothed her, healed her.

Even a simple invitation to go for coffee would've been welcome. He wanted them to move on but could she? After seeing him again, she couldn't deny the flame for Matt still burned inside her. The disappointment was crushing. *I knew you were angry. I figured it out, later. I've been waiting for you to find me. Now this...a polite note and goodbye forever. Even after last night? I've never loved anyone like I love you.*

Sobbing, she lowered her head down on the table. Perri swore she'd cried every tear she had for Mikey...now she was crying for herself and couldn't stop. Lacy returned to find Perri running to the stairs.

The older woman put down her bag before she picked up Matt's note. After a few minutes, she put her palm to her chin, then muttered, "Dear me."

Up in her room, Perri flung herself on the bed. After fifteen minutes of unstoppable tears, she sat up to grab the tissue box. *We didn't know each other very well...not long, not long enough. Matt, I've missed you so much...needed you so much. Now even my smallest hope for us is gone. Why didn't you say this sooner? Why didn't you come to me...why did this happen to us?*

* * * *

Matt paced in his new little house. The flowers had been delivered with his note over an hour ago yet she hadn't appeared. He wanted—no, he needed for her to accept his apology. He had said terrible, terrible things to her that night. Sure, she fired off some pretty good shots too. But he knew she was angry, she didn't mean it. Then she ran off and filed for divorce. He shook his head. *The last thing I wanted was a divorce from you. I needed you but you threw me out in the cold. You've moved on. I love you too much to hold you back.*

Matt went into the living room, picked up the drill, then put it down. He paced, looked at his list of things to do but couldn't concentrate. *Perri, where are you? I still need you...need you to forgive me. Is there anything left between us?*

Matt sat brooding over a cup of coffee when he heard the front door of the house next door slam. He peered out the living room window and saw Perri striding by, right in front of his house.

Now's my chance! Matt jumped up nearly spilling his coffee to run for the door. His long legs caught up with her easily. He fell into her rhythm. *Now what? Be direct. She always liked that.*

"Did you get my flowers?" He noticed she wore running shoes.

"Yes, thank you." Her gaze remained straight ahead.

"And the note?"

"I did."

He halted in the middle of the street and grabbed her upper arm to spin her around.

"That's all you have to say?" The note of irritation in his voice was unmistakable.

As she stood in front of him, he ached to take her in his arms. She seemed so strong. *Perri's usual façade.* But her expression gave her away. He saw emotion flash across her face, pain, agony, exhaustion. His arm moved involuntarily toward her but he stopped it halfway.

"What do you want me to say?" She rested her hands on her hips.

He stood looking at her, seeing the ache in her eyes but he didn't know what to do.

"Do you forgive me?"

"Of course. I forgave you a long time ago. I said some pretty terrible things too."

"I forgave you…at the time, actually." He glanced down at his hands, then back at her.

"But you stormed out." She cocked her head slightly.

"Needed some air, some distance. With my out of control anger…what I said to you…I didn't trust myself. I left to-to protect you from more harsh words or actions from me. I wasn't safe to be around."

"That's why you left?" Her eyebrows shot up.

"Of course. What did you think?" He stepped closer to her, placing his hands on her arms.

"I thought…I thought…" He saw her struggle for the right words.

"What? Spit it out."

"I thought you left because you were through...didn't love me or want to be with me anymore." Her reply was barely audible. Blinking rapidly wasn't enough to hold back her tears.

"How could you think that? How could I ever stop loving you?" he whispered, staring into her eyes.

With his words, Perri broke down. Matt gathered her into his arms. She sobbed into his chest, unable to stop. He stroked her hair, letting her cry while his eyes misted.

"So you're saying..." Perri sputtered out when she could take a breath.

He felt heat rise to his cheeks. *Time to step up. Man up, Marine. Tell her the truth.*

"Saying I still love you. I took a vow. I meant it. You may not want me, but I'll never stop loving you."

"Not want you? I can barely keep my hands off you." She looked up at him.

That's all he needed to hear. Matt lowered his mouth to hers, tentatively at first. When she parted her lips, he took her mouth as he crushed her to his chest. Pent-up passion exploded inside Matt, coursing through his veins at lightning speed. He broke from her, took her arm and whisked them into his house.

Once the door was closed, they attacked each other, frantically ripping clothes from each other's bodies, stopping only for a deep kiss to stoke the fires. When they were naked, Matt held her at arm's length while his gaze raked her body.

"So beautiful. God, I've missed you...looking at you...touching you."

"Me too. Hold me one more time, please?"

She flattened her palms on his chest as he wound his arms around her, pulling her to him for a possessive kiss. He backed them up until his legs hit the sofa. Turning, he lowered her gently onto the cushions. She folded her fingers around his arm to pull him down on top of her. Propped up on his knees, Matt closed his hands around her breasts.

"Still a perfect fit," he mumbled.

Perri's hands traced his shoulders while he massaged her. He kissed her neck, moving up by inches toward the soft spot behind her ear. *Wonder if that's still a huge turn-on for her.* He nibbled there until she moaned, squirming under him.

"You remembered..." she murmured.

"Still your favorite, eh?" he whispered. "How could I forget one inch of your body?"

Perri wrapped her leg around his waist, bringing him closer. He lowered his head, closing his lips on her peak to lick, then suck.

"Still the greatest."

"Even after childbirth?" She ran her hand through his hair.

"Hell, yeah." He bent his head again.

* * * *

Perri curled her fingers around his arms, sliding up to cup his powerful shoulders. Matt still knew how to arouse her—zero to one hundred miles an hour in less than a minute. Five years of pent-up want being freed created a heat in her body she could barely stand. When he moved his hand up her thigh to her wet center, she groaned.

"Matt, please. I want you."

"Not yet. I'm not through playin'. I've waited five years, not hurrying now."

"Oh, God, I'm going to come." Perri was pleading.

"Go ahead. I like to watch you. Then do it again and again."

"Sadist!" She laughed.

Perri could feel her orgasm building. She reached down to wrap her fingers around his shaft. He was as hard as steel. His fingers stroked her, searching until they found the right spot. Her body undulated under his deft touch. She stroked Matt in a rhythm that elicited a groan from him.

"Hey, no fair," he muttered, dislodging her hand.

He thrust two fingers into her, bringing her to climax. Her hips lifted off the sofa as every muscle in her body tensed. A cry escaped her throat, her eyes closed while pleasure rocketed to every part of her body. When she opened her eyes, Matt was staring at her with an amused expression on his face.

"Beautiful in ecstasy...as always." He chuckled.

Heat rose to her cheeks but instead of responding, she reached for him.

His hand blocked hers. "Ah, ah, I don't think so. I'm only human. When I go baby, it's going to be inside of you."

He mounted her, entering with a quick thrust. She lifted her knee higher to allow him to fill her completely. He groaned loudly as he pushed up all the way.

"Oh, Matt! God, it's so good." Perri buried her face in his shoulder.

"Baby...baby...baby, you're...incredible," he uttered, moving his hips in a slow rhythm.

He made love to her as if no time had passed—as if they had made love just the day before. Matt pushed up to look into her eyes. Perri saw the loving expression she had always seen when they made love. The way he looked at her warmed her heart. His gentle sexiness aroused her again. She felt desire building. She kissed him, then cupped his rough cheek with her palm.

"I love you so much," she whispered.

"Oh God, baby. Tell me again." His eyes closed.

"I love you...for always."

Matt picked up his rhythm. Perri noticed the flush of sexual excitement stealing up his neck, signaling he'd soon climax. He was moving faster now, grunting, closing his eyes, then opening them again.

"I love you, Perri...forever."

Then he was lost in an explosive orgasm that stole his breath. He whimpered as his body shuddered on top of hers. Lost in her second orgasm, Perri almost missed his.

They lay panting, holding each other, skin to slippery, sweaty skin. Love filled Perri's heart, making her feel safe and happy. His hands played with her hair. She planted tiny kisses on his shoulder.

"I need you, Perri," he whispered into her hair.

"I need you too."

He sat back on his haunches, pulling out of her.

"So what are we going to do about it?" he asked, his hands slowly caressing her chest.

"What do you suggest?" She touched his cheek.

He sat still, staring at her, his gaze roving over her body.

"A bit hard to concentrate with you looking like that right in front of me."

"Hey, you're a Marine. A little self-control." He chuckled. "I think we ought to get married."

Her eyes widened. "What?"

"You heard me. Get married. Now. Today. Here."
"Again?"
He nodded.
Perri fell into a fit of laughing as if she were being tickled.
"What's so funny?" Matt was clearly annoyed.
"Déjà vu all over again!" She ran her forefinger down his chest.
"That's redundant."
"Yeah, I know." She slid her fingers through his chest hair.
"Are you saying you won't marry me?" His brows knitted.
"I'm saying, I will."
A huge grin broke out on his face.
She smiled up at him.
"Today—now—we have so little time." Matt maneuvered himself to stand up. He offered her his hand.
"Okay. Shower first, then dress?"
"Shower…together? We'll never get to the judge's."
He snickered.

* * * *

After making love again in the shower, they dressed, then climbed in her car.
"We need to iron out a few things first," Perri said, steering the car toward Oak Bend.
"I'm starved. Let's stop at Sadie's Place."
Sadie's daughter, Marie, seated the couple. They ordered, then sat back.
"Okay. Start the negotiation." Matt sat back, sipping his coffee.
"Positive attitude, please."
He waved his hand at her. "You're right. Sorry. Go ahead."
"We can't start out like we did before with no plan. First, where are we going to live?" Perri sat back and picked up her mug while she gazed at Matt.
"I promised myself a thousand times, if I got a second chance with you, I'd quit Afghanistan and return stateside. North Carolina would be my preference. Would you agree to that?"

"Leave my job in Manhattan for North Carolina?" She saw him tense. "That works for me. Learning to compromise here." *I'd move anywhere to be with you.*

She chuckled at the look of relief on his face.

"How long will it take you to do that?"

"Don't know. But I'll apply for it as soon as I return."

Their food arrived. They tucked into Reuben sandwiches with enthusiasm.

"One more deal breaker," she said before taking another bite of her sandwich.

"Deal breaker? Are we looking for ways to deep-six this?" Matt put his food down.

"Bad choice of words...one more thing I want."

"Shoot." He picked up his sandwich again.

"No more children." Perri's fingers unfolded, then refolded her napkin.

"What?" He almost spit out his food.

"You heard. I can't do it again. Can't lose another child."

"I've felt the same...but if I were around...we were together...it might not happen again."

"Don't want to risk it. You need to get a vasectomy." She toyed with the food on her plate.

"What!" He put his sandwich down.

"You heard—"

"Wait a minute. I didn't think I wanted another child either...but if it were with you. That's different." He reached for her hand, closing his fingers around hers.

"I'm scared." Perri's voice was almost a whisper. She put her fork down and gazed out the window.

"I know, baby. Hey, it might already be too late."

Her head snapped back, her eyes grew wide as the truth of his words sunk in.

"Oh my God. I hadn't thought about that. We-we didn't...oh God!" She put her head in her hands.

His hand wrapped around her forearm, his thumb lightly rubbed her skin.

"We'll be together. If you are, it'll be great. I want that...want to have another child with you." His soft voice caressed her, soothed her.

She looked up.

"But what if?" Worry furrowed her brow.

"Shhh." He put his finger on her lips. "Don't even think about it. You're probably not. Let's go ahead with our plans. We can talk about kids after we're married, living in North Carolina...together."

They ate in silence for a while. Perri's mind was a tornado of thoughts, fears, worries, happiness all mixed together. Matt's happy face reassured her. *Can we do it this time? Can we make it work? Will we hurt each other again? I couldn't take it a second time. But I love him...don't want to live another minute without him.*

"Okay. I'm done here. Let's get married." Matt put his napkin on the table.

"What about...what if—"

"None of that!"

"But—"

"No! We love each other. We have to trust we'll find a way to work it out, Perri. I don't want to go on without you anymore...it seems you feel the same."

She nodded.

"So let's get married." Matt grabbed the check.

He paid at the front by the door. Perri placed her small hand in his as they walked out together.

"Do you remember the judge?" she asked Matt as they got in the car.

"Damn right I do. Judge George Wainwright, 23 Central Street in Oak Bend. Drive lady."

Perri chuckled as she put the car in gear.

* * * *

After the judge waived the two-day waiting period to marry them, Perri and Matt celebrated by dining at the fanciest restaurant in the county, Chez Pierre, a French bistro in Oak Bend. Perri couldn't believe she was Mrs. Matt Jessup again. She kept expecting to wake up to find her happiness was only a dream. They held hands over dinner gazing at each other like newlyweds. The waiter brought a piece of special cake as a gift to the bride and groom.

Matt carried her over the threshold of the small house all the way into the bedroom where he dumped her on the bed. He eased down on top of her, devouring her mouth with his. The couple could barely get undressed before coupling in a frenzy born of five years of thwarted desire. Perri unleashed her hunger for him as he thrust into her hard, making her cry out with pleasure. Matt's control broke when Perri's hips arched up during her climax. He groaned loudly as he plunged into her again and again.

Sweat dripped off Matt's forehead onto the pillow next to Perri's head. He kissed her tenderly while her hands caressed his shoulders.

"You're amazing," he said, rolling off her to the side.

She cuddled up against him, resting her head and hand on his chest. Matt's arm circled her, drawing her closer.

"So are you."

"I've never had a woman like you, before or since."

"Oh? How many have you had since?" Perri sat up.

"Don't go there, woman." Matt drew her to him again.

"What will we do with this adorable house?"

"Let's keep fixing it up. We can come here when I get leave, especially in the summer time when it's hotter 'an Hell in North Carolina."

"I love this house. It has potential. Love what you've done so far."

He brushed her lips with his.

"I love it too. Our house…and Mikey's too."

Perri hugged him.

* * * *

The next day the newlyweds stuck together like glue. Perri moved her things from Lacy Ryan's Guesthouse into Matt's house. The warm morning morphed into a blistering hot afternoon. The little house had no air conditioning so the lovers sat in the shade in their small yard, drinking iced tea. It was too hot even to work on the house…but not too hot to make love in the cool sheets on their cozy bed.

"Let's make love in the lake tonight, after dark," Matt whispered in Perri's ear as they sat on folding chairs under the protection of a tall elm tree in the front yard.

"Sounds like a plan."

Dinner outside at Homer's was a bit more comfortable as there was some breeze from the lake. Matt and Perri had their heads together, making plans for their living quarters in North Carolina.

"We can visit on Skype on the computer while I'm away," Matt said.

"I've never done that."

"I'll show you how."

They spent the afternoon going over how to Skype as well as choosing colors to paint their living room in North Carolina, if that ever came to pass.

Darkness brought welcome cooling but the night air remained heavy with humidity. Matt and Perri stole silently down to the dock at ten o'clock.

"Let's meet in the middle," Perri said, slipping out of her jersey shift.

"You've been naked under that all evening?"

"You didn't notice?"

"I must be brain-dead." He chuckled.

"Too hot for panties. You're a better swimmer. Give me a head start."

Not waiting for his reply, Perri raced off the end of the dock and dove into the water stark naked. She was a good strong swimmer but not as fast as Matt who swam competitively in high school. He ran back to the house to drop off his wallet. When he returned, Perri was more than halfway to the middle of the lake. He started to take off his shoes when he heard the low rumble. A storm was coming in fast. The thunder grew louder rapidly. Matt looked for Perri's head above the water. He caught a glimpse of her in the moonlight, she was almost to the middle of the lake. Then he saw it...his blood ran cold. A few seconds after the loud crack of thunder, a vein of bright white lightning sliced through the black of the night. Matt saw Perri stop bobbing up and start treading water as rain began to fall from the sky.

Another clap of thunder followed almost immediately by another jagged line of lightning cutting through the darkness.

Water conducts electricity, the lake was the most dangerous place for Perri to be. Fear mobilized Matt.

Shit! Perri! I can't lose you too. I can't!

Matt's military training kicked in. He focused on rescue, stuffing his fears and emotion away. He ripped off his shirt, shorts, then shoes in case he had to swim. Grabbing the rope and a towel lying on the dock, he leapt into the rowboat nearly capsizing it. The thunder rolled in as lightning split the sky. Matt gripped the oars and began to row. At first his muscles felt the resistance of the water, but then adrenaline kicked in. His strength increased, enabling him to slice the oars through the water rapidly. He turned to look for Perri but didn't see her. Rain continued to fall faster and harder, obscuring his vision.

He allowed the boat to drift for a few minutes while his eyes scanned the water. Finally, he saw her head bob up. He called to her while waving his arms but the thunder drowned out his voice. Matt returned to the oars, guiding the boat over the choppy waters toward Perri. He'd stroke and stroke, then stop to look for Perri. He couldn't tell if she knew he was in the boat or not or if she could even see the boat in the pitch black. When the next bolt of lightning hit, it lit up the sky. Matt took the opportunity to wave frantically with both hands, hoping to catch Perri's eye.

This last time he succeeded. She raised a hand about a foot out of the water back at him. The rain was almost a solid sheet now. He was soaked, his hands slipped on the oars, the towel was wet through. He cupped his hands to yell at her to stay where she was but she didn't hear him. He returned to rowing, his arms increased the pace until he caught up with her. Pulling the oars up, he drifted closer to her, trying not to hit her with the boat. He heard his name from the other side of the boat. He leapt across the small craft. As he reached over the side his hand made contact with flesh. *Perri's hand!*

Running on automatic pilot, he jerked her closer until he could cup his big hands under her armpits. He hauled her into the boat in one motion. She was breathing heavily when he kissed her quickly, then jumped back to the oars.

"We're on borrowed time, being the tallest thing on this lake. If one bolt hits this boat, we're both toast."

Matt focused all his energy on rowing. Perri wrapped the drenched towel around her naked, wet, trembling body. He took a deep breath while using only one oar to turn the boat around. Once it was facing shore, he focused his energy and rowed as fast as he could. Matt tightened his grip on the slippery oars, causing the wood to rip through the skin of his palms. Pain shot through his hands, then zoomed up his arms, but he kept rowing. A warm liquid dripped down his fingers but he didn't stop. The boat fairly flew through the water. Thunder continued to crash however the time elapsed between thunder and lightning gradually grew longer, indicating the storm was moving off.

They came crashing into the dock at breakneck speed. He threw the rope loop over the hook on the dock before he helped Perri up. Matt hauled himself up, then pulled a shivering Perri close to him. One more low rumble was followed by a brilliant flash of lightning hitting a tree nearby with a loud *crack*. The couple jumped back. Perri took Matt's hand as they ran for the little house. Inside, he closed the door, then leaned his back against it, breathing heavily. Once the danger was over, his body reacted. He trembled and his eyes watered when Perri hugged his waist. Matt tried to catch his breath.

"You saved me."

"If anything had happened to you..." He stopped, overcome with emotion.

She held him until his shaking stopped.

"It didn't. I'm safe now."

"You're freezing."

Perri opened his hand. Blood.

"Let's get these bandaged," she said, leading him to the bathroom.

* * * *

Matt and Perri had a tearful parting two days after the storm. Each headed their separate way, vowing to write, Skype or email whenever they could. The agony of leaving Matt knifed through her heart. The exhilaration of knowing they'd be together calmed her. She glanced at the plain gold band on her finger whenever she doubted their commitment. The third night back, Matt was on Skype with her.

"The guys congratulated me, then got all goofy about the fact that my new bride was you."

"No one here even asked me about it. That's fine. Less to explain. How are your hands?"

"Getting better. I put through the transfer papers. Fingers crossed, baby."

She smiled at him.

"Love you."

They blew kisses at each other before signing off. The next two weeks seemed to fly until Perri started feeling sick. She took the dreaded home pregnancy test right before a scheduled Skype session with Matt.

"You said a surprise?" he asked.

"I took a home pregnancy test about fifteen minutes ago."

"And?"

"I waited until we were together to read the results."

Perri disappeared for a moment while she retreated to the bathroom. She returned with the stick, then held it up to the screen.

"Pink. What does that mean?" His brows knitted.

"I'm pregnant." Perri burst into tears.

"It's gonna be all right, Perri. You'll see. I'll be there this time."

"Sure, sure. That's what you said—"

"Stop! Don't go there. No more *last time* shit, baby. I will."

* * * *

Time passed slowly for Perri. Eventually she had to tell her boss she was pregnant. It wasn't well received. *I hate working here anyway.* Perri negotiated a deal with them to get extended severance and maternity leave if she agreed not to come back. She left two weeks before her due date. Communication with Matt had been spotty in the two months prior because of his missions. She worried when she didn't hear from him. *Just my luck to have the baby survive but lose the father.* Perri pushed that thought out of her head as it scared her to death.

The Call of Duty

The day came a week later than expected. Her bag was packed early as Perri was efficient. When her water broke she sent an email to Matt, took her bag and waddled down the stairs to find a taxi. Fortunately a young couple gave her their cab. As Perri rode to the hospital her nerves began to fray.

* * * *

The message got to Matt but not in time to talk with her before she left. He was frantic about her welfare, being a week overdo. His commanding officer granted him an emergency leave. A military plane flew him to the base in North Carolina where he had to transfer to a commercial flight.

He worried the entire way about her health. Frightening images of her or the baby dying kept popping into his mind. His stomach was in a knot, his appetite went south.

* * * *

Back at Eastern New York Hospital, Perri was prepped for a C-section since a vaginal birth didn't appear to be a possibility. They tried induction but her cervix didn't dilate enough though she kept having contractions. Perri was losing her nerve. *Matt, where are you?*

Hour after hour passed as the doctors waited for her body to respond. Twelve hours later they determined a C-section was necessary. The doctors began prep. Perri was half out of her mind worrying about the baby, terrified to go through the experience alone. Her parents had died five years earlier, one from a heart attack, then the other from cancer. Though Perri was thirty-two, she felt like a little girl who needed her mama.

After the epidural was administered they wheeled her into the operating room.

She used the Lamaze breathing techniques she learned to calm herself down. The panting left her a little lightheaded. She gripped the table hard as she stared straight at the completely covered person coming toward her. *I'm hallucinating. They've given me dangerous drugs.* She opened her mouth to scream but no sound came out because someone was kissing her. *I think it's a man but in the green suit, white mask and green shower cap...can't tell. Might've been kissed by a woman...a very big woman.*

"I'm here, baby."

The voice is familiar. I'm dreaming. Matt's voice. Wake up, Perri.

"Perri? Perri?" He shook her gently until she became alert again.

She looked up into his eyes.

"Yeah, baby. It's me. I made it." His eyes crinkled with his grin.

"Matt?"

He nodded, slipping his mask down again so she could see his face.

"You're really here?"

"I'm here. We're in this together."

The doctor and nurse put the drape up. Matt stepped back around to the other side of the table.

"I'll be right here the whole time, honey. Hang on. Baby's almost here."

Perri's eyes teared.

"Don't cry, sister. This'll be a piece of cake," the nurse said, touching her shoulder.

Perri felt Matt's hand take hers. She closed her eyes, exhausted.

* * * *

The sound of a baby crying woke up Perri. Matt was holding their baby while the doctors were stitching her up.

"Fine baby girl, Perri. Nice job!" Matt leaned down to kiss her through his mask.

"A girl?"

"Yup, with all her fingers and toes."

Perri smiled, shifting her eyes to Matt and the baby.

"What do you want to call her?" he asked.

"Michelle?"

"Good. Baby Michelle. I like it." He rocked slightly, keeping the baby steady in the crook of his large arm.

Perri watched him stare down lovingly at their child. *He was right. We had to do this.* Goose bumps tingled down her arms. The doctors finished with her, then wheeled her back to her room. Things happened quickly. Before she knew it, the baby was asleep in a tiny bassinet next to her bed. Matt, dressed in his uniform, sat on her bed holding her hand.

"She's going to be beautiful like you," he whispered.

"Think so?"

He nodded.

"But what if—"

"Stop!" He held up his hand. "Don't go there. I'm here. This time I'm not leaving. If we have to stand watch night and day, we will. She will survive. Trust me, Perri."

"I do, Matt."

"Love you, baby."

"Love you too."

* * * *

The following summer, Matt, Perri and Michelle drove all the way from North Carolina to their house in tiny Pine Grove. They took Michelle out on the lake to celebrate Mikey's birthday because mothers and fathers never forget.

THE END

Love After All
Sandy Sullivan
Copyright © 2012

Chapter One

The satiny slide of silk caressing her left nipple, made her breath catch in her throat. Wayne's lips followed the material, soft, wet across her breast. He knew exactly what to do to make her want him. How he did it, Maggie didn't know, but he always seemed to bring out the best and the worst in her, at least from the moment they hooked up again.

The glare of the Vegas lights illuminated the expensive hotel room from the line of windows encompassing one whole wall. No Motel Six for Wayne Ridges. Only the best would do. Penthouse suite, open bar with more liquor than the best cowboy bars in Houston and silk sheets on the bed. Things a top bullrider could afford boggled her mind—luxuries she could only hope to have one day. The room had a huge king sized bed near the bank of windows with a separate living area where one could dine, drink or sit back and watch television if they so chose. Color from the flashing neon lights on the strip, bounced off the white walls of the room, capturing her attention. Flash. Dark. Flash. Dark. The rhythmic pattern of the lights hypnotized her as thoughts of where they would go once this little rendezvous ended, clouded her mind.

"You're thinkin' too much, Maggie."

"Sorry."

"What'cha thinkin' about?" he asked right before his mouth closed over her nipple. Blue eyes glanced up through thick dark lashes. At six foot four and all muscle, the man could stop traffic on a bad day or cause an accident on a good.

Not ready to tell him exactly where her thoughts drifted, she said, "You and what you do to me. You can wind me up like a top."

He slowly drew her nipple into his mouth with a steady pull as his hand crept down her abdomen heading for the place she needed his touch like her next breath.

The suction on her breast made her hips surge up when his fingers found the tiny nub of her sex. *God, the man is good.* Fingers parted her pussy lips to give him better access to the place he sought. She knew from experience with Wayne, it wouldn't take much to have her soaring amongst the clouds.

They'd been together for the last two weeks but their time was coming to an end. She had to return to duty while he would return home. Her unit would be shipping out for Afghanistan in two days for an eighteen month tour. She didn't want to go, but her job called. Normal duty for her meant sheet metal work on jet fighters coming in and out of Nellis Airforce Base. Days on end of riveting, grinding and painting. Most people found her job funny since normally a man would be in this type of position. She didn't.

"Am I that boring, Maggie?"

"What?" Startled out of her reverence, she said, "No, why would you say something so demeaning?"

"Your mind is wandering off while I'm makin' love to you. I obviously can't hold your attention."

"Yes you are, Wayne. I love being with you."

"Babe, what's botherin' you?" he asked, propping himself up on his elbow. Blue eyes framed by long eyelashes stared up at her with sincerity clear in his gaze.

She wondered what would have happened had they not hooked up at Cowboy Corner two weeks ago. Their past didn't enter into the mix of their time together now. Hooking up after years of growing up in the same town…people wouldn't believe it if she told them. Wayne had any girl he wanted in high school. She was a band geek. He didn't go out with her type.

Why they had hooked up now, she wasn't sure, but she did have to admit, after contacts and braces, she cleaned up pretty nice these days. She liked her brown hair, green eyes and long legs. Her abdomen could use some work, but those sit-ups were helping. She had to stay in fairly good shape being in the military, but they provided great workouts. She didn't do everything she could to stay in shape though.

Trepidation slipped down her back with each breath she took over this deployment. What would happen after Wayne left for home? Would they continue to see each other on a long term basis? She didn't think so. This wasn't a relationship kind of thing happening between them. A few nights of great sex, a few dates at the PBR parties he had to attend…nothing more.

"I'm kind of afraid of this tour. I have a bad feeling about it."

"Everythin' will be fine."

"I don't think so, Wayne." She pushed herself up against the headboard, leaving him closer to the middle of the bed. "I don't want to cause waves here, but what happens when National Finals Rodeo is over?"

"What do you mean?"

"You go back to Shipley. I go overseas amongst flying bullets. I realize this isn't anything to you except a quick hook up, which is fine with me. I'd just like to know where we stand."

"You won't be around bullets, will you?" he asked, the sincerity now turning to worry.

"I could be, Wayne. I'm not sure what everything is going to be like over there. I'm scared."

"Come here," he said, crawling up to the top of the bed to wrap a beefy arm around her shoulders. "You'll be fine, darlin'."

Her cheek found the hard muscles of his pecs as she snuggled to his side.

"There. All better."

She giggled while rolling on top of him.

"Now, this I could get into."

"Everything is about sex with you," she said as she rolled her eyes and propped herself up on her elbow.

"Shouldn't it be? I'm a man." His hands settled on her waist then slowly crept up her sides until his thumbs rested beneath her breasts.

"True enough. No one could think you were anything else with the hard flesh pressing into my belly."

"All for you, babe. After all, we were in the middle of making love before this conversation started."

"True. Shall we start over?"

"Mmm. As long as you promise to stay with me this time."

"And if I don't?" she teased, shifting her hips from side to side so his cock rubbed her along her belly. There's nothing like hard man flesh to make her wet, especially if it came in the form of Wayne Ridges.

"I'll eat you out until you scream for me to stop. I'll make you come so many times you can't stand it anymore."

Her clit throbbed with each beat of her heart, flooding her pussy with cream. She wanted this man badly. Two weeks of hot sex only made her need him more. "That is supposed to deter me? Sounds like something I might enjoy."

"Oh really?"

"Um." She glanced up through her lashes and tilted her head. "Yeah."

Faster than she could blink, he had her beneath him. "You're on, babe."

The feel of his mouth drove her wild. Goose bumps flittered across her skin, trailing after the path of his lips, down her neck, across her shoulder, licking and nipping as he went. His mouth closed for her nipple and drew it deep into his mouth.

"Please, Wayne." She arched her back, pushing her breast further into his mouth.

"What do you want, Maggie mine?"

Yours? Am I really? She couldn't believe that. Not for a minute. Guys like Wayne didn't settle down. They didn't fall in love with a girl like her. "Love me."

"With everything I have."

He swept down her body like a tidal wave against the shore, pushing aside her thoughts and insecurities until she couldn't think beyond what his mouth was doing as he settled himself between her thighs. The brush of his tongue against her clit tore a moan from her lips. "God, Wayne."

His hum of approval vibrated against her pussy.

Stroke after stroke, lick after lick. Everything he did made her want him buried inside her. The thought of his hard flesh pushed deep brought her hips up. A slow bump and grind of her pussy against his mouth drove her desire to its peak until she cried out in ecstasy.

"There we go," he whispered as a grin spread across his lips. "That sounded more like someone who is into this sex thing."

"You are such a jerk sometimes," she said, smacking his shoulder.

A soft moan echoed around the room as he buried his cock deep in her pussy with one snap of his hips. "What were you saying?"

"Nothin'."

"I thought not."

The slow glide of his cock in and out had her eyes rolling back in her head as a deep sigh escaping her lips. "God, you feel good, Wayne."

"It's only a cock, babe."

"Your cock feels incredible."

"Glad you like it."

In and out. Hard steel covered in silk. His skin branded her with every pass. The feel of his hair roughed thighs brushing the softer flesh of her own, drew goose bumps on her legs. He pulled out amidst her disappointed sigh.

"Don't worry, I'm not done yet. Roll over," he said, smacking her thigh.

She scooted up, rolled over and got up on her knees. Him fucking her from behind made her girly parts tingle as her body ached for more. She wanted him to ass-fuck her. The feel of him deep in her ass…mmm. There's nothing like his cock buried in that dark, forbidden tunnel.

"Where did the lube go?"

"In the nightstand drawer," she replied, wiggling her butt.

The slide of the drawer reminded her of the toys in the bottom. A rabbit vibrator. Nipple clamps. A butt-plug. Handcuffs. Wayne liked to play rough sometimes, but everything he'd done so far made her hotter than a firecracker on the Fourth of July.

"I want to tie you to the bed except I need your ass more."

"Good because the feeling of you buried there drives me crazy." Cool lube plopped near the pucker of her anus. "Damn, that's cold."

"Sorry, babe."

"No, you aren't."

"You're right. I'm not. It makes your rosy little hole pucker for me."

"Bastard." A moan escaped her lips as he pushed one finger past the ring of muscles.

"More?"

"Fuck yes."

"Do you want my cock?"

"Please."

The moment the head of his dick popped past the ring of muscles in her ass, she groaned and closed her eyes. A slight burn pushed a hiss past her lips.

"Okay?"

"Yes. Do it. I want all of you." She rested her forehead on the bed. Seconds later, she could feel his pubic hair brush her butt cheeks and knew he was deep in her ass. "God, that's incredible, Wayne. So full."

Wayne's breathing sawed from between his lips in short pants. She could tell he held on by the skin of his cock as he tried to forestall the impending explosion of cum. His hands shook where they held on to her hips.

"Are you all right?"

"Yeah. I'm just trying—" he whispered with a groan, "to not come so fast, but your ass is scalding me."

"Fuck me, Wayne. Give me everything you got cowboy. Ride this cowgirl more than eight seconds."

"I'm not so sure if I have more than eight seconds in me, babe, but I'll give it a try."

His hips shifted back, then forward. If felt like heaven and hell at the same time. Her ass burned with the stretch, but she wanted more. She wanted everything he would give, but also everything he wasn't prepared to fork over.

She wanted his heart.

Chapter Two

Jets flew overhead with a roaring whoosh as Maggie rubbed her gritty eyes. She hated Afghanistan and everything the godforsaken place stood for. The constant alertness they maintained got on her nerves with each passing day. Every time another body came back from a patrol wounded or dead, she prayed she would return home in one piece. Why in the hell did she ever join the military in the first place? Oh yeah. To pay off loans and have a decent job when she got out. The job she loved, it was the hell they put them through every day that she hated.

"MacPherson?"

"Yeah," she hollered back from the wheel well of the fighter jet she was working on.

"Mail call. You got a letter."

"Thanks." She glanced at the return address when her sergeant handed her the envelope and her heart leapt with joy.

Wayne.

After their time in Vegas, they parted with sweet words of thanks and see ya around, nothing to indicate if he felt anything at all. He'd written a couple of times in the six months she'd been over here telling her about the off-season at home working on his parent's ranch and giving her the lowdown on the people of Shipley. Never once did he mention feelings. Did he care at all? It sure didn't seem like it.

The strong scent of aftershave drifted up to her nose from the envelope. His letters always smelled so good. Just like he did the last time they'd made love. She wouldn't think of it as fucking now that their time together was over. Making love could be anything from petting to actual penetration and she wanted to keep all those feelings he stirred deep within her heart. Would she see him again? What would he say when they met after so much time apart? Hi. How ya doin'? Wanna fuck? Yeah, he probably would. Their time together in Vegas meant nothing to him. He'd made it clear from the beginning he wasn't the kind to have a steady girlfriend these days and with them thousands of miles apart, things wouldn't work anyway. The infamous Wayne Ridges didn't do relationships.

Her thoughts drifted while she finished her shift. The day was almost over and she could read her letter in the relative privacy of her bunk in a few short minutes. First chow, then shower, then letter, in that order.

Even though the hangar she worked at was very remote, she felt safe enough to walk without an escort to the barracks she shared with the other few women on this base. They didn't hear about too much trouble with insurgents shooting at women, but one never knew.

The blood red sun began its slow decent into the nighttime sky leaving her ready to call it a day. The latest patrol said to be careful tonight. They'd found signs of snipers not too far away on their morning rounds. All had been quiet during the afternoon.

Maggie finished putting everything away and slowly pushed her tired body toward the open bay doors. Their makeshift workshop didn't give them much except cover from the scorching sun during the day and the blasting sand during a storm. Other than that, they worked hot, sweaty and gritty until they could shower away the day's grime.

Everything seemed too quiet as she made her way across the compound toward the mess tent. Nothing stirred, not even a hint of a breeze.

A sharp crack exploded on the night air and a searing pain exploded in her left leg as she went down, hitting her head on the hard ground.

"Sniper!"

The base burst into the frenzy of running people.

"Where are you hit?" a medic asked, crouching down next to her.

"My leg. Fuck!"

"Oh hell."

"What?"

"Nothin'. Hang tight. We'll get you to safety. The guards are already headed out to find the sniper."

"Just get me somewhere where I can pass out. I hit my head when I went down. I've got a fucking headache from hell."

"You'll be fine. Just hang with me," he said, rolling some gauze around her knee to stop the bleeding she assumed, while she tried hard not to vomit.

She didn't do blood. "I'm hanging dude."

Her world started to spin, then everything went black.

* * * *

The plane touched down in Shipley jarring her in her seat. *Damn, my knee is killing me.* The small plane she had to take from Houston didn't leave much room for her to stretch out her leg so the cramped position she had to keep it in didn't help the stiffness. Her mother and father promised to meet her at the airport to help her get home.

"Home. What the hell am I gonna do here?"

Recuperate, dummy.

Her inner voice had been giving her hell ever since the accident. She'd hated Afghanistan and dreaded being there for another year. God in his infinite wisdom stepped in to send her home even if it was with a shattered knee, busted up leg and a decision to make.

"Hang tight. We'll get the chair for you to get down the stairs in."

"I can make it on my crutches."

"The stairs are very steep. It would be better with the chair."

A deep voice broke into her thoughts, scattering what little brain power she had left. "I got her." Strong arms picked her up out of the seat and cradled her next to his chest.

"Wayne."

"Hey, babe. Got yourself a bit banged up I see," he said, looking down into her eyes.

She couldn't breathe much less form a coherent thought.

"Let's get you out of here and comfortable."

"What are you doin' here?" she asked, finding her voice finally.

"I came to get you. Told your parents I'd handle pickin' you up and gettin' you back home." He eased them down the three small stairs of the plane and onto the tarmac. "I'd rather carry you to my truck, but I brought the wheelchair in case you'd rather ride."

"I'll ride in the chair, thanks."

"Party pooper," he said, gently sitting her in the chair. "Your chauffer awaits, my lady."

What she assumed to be his truck sat several feet away, in all its glory. A silver, shiny brand new F150 pickup. "Nice ride."

"Thanks. It was my present to myself for winning the world championship last year." She squeaked as he scooped her up in his arms. This sure wasn't how she'd hoped to see him again or be held in his arms. "Get the door?"

She reached over and grabbed the handle to pull the door open while he backed up.

"I guess I should have opened it before I picked you up."

"You didn't have to pick me up even. I could have got in with my crutches."

"I like holding you."

"You do?" she asked, not sure what he might have meant by that.

"Sure. Just because I haven't seen you in a while, doesn't mean I don't want you, Maggie."

"But you never said…"

"What?"

"Nothin'. Never mind."

He slid her inside the cab before he buckled her seatbelt. "We need to talk, but now isn't the time."

After he slammed the door shut and tucked the wheelchair in the back of his vehicle, he walked around the front of the truck as she watched through the windshield. He hadn't changed much since Vegas. She wasn't sure what to expect really. It had only been six month since she'd seen him and he still looked good enough to eat. Hair to his collar and big blue eyes. Hard chest. Flat abs. *Damn the man had it all.*

"I have to say one thing."

"What's that?" she asked once he'd settled himself behind the wheel.

"Did you get my last letter?"

"Yes."

"Good."

Yeah, she'd received it but she wasn't sure where it was anymore. The envelope had been in her shirt pocket the day of her accident.

He started the truck and shifted into drive. "I take it you want me to take you to your parent's place."

"Uh, where else would you take me?"

"My place maybe."

Now, she really was confused. What the hell did he write in that letter?

"I um…"

"No rushing. I'll take you to your parent's house. We don't need to talk about things until you get settled."

All his talk really had her baffled. He almost sounded like he…*gulp*…cared.

They rode in silence for several minutes while she tried desperately to think of where his letter might be. Still in her shirt pocket? In her duffle?

She wasn't sure what to say and he seemed content to just be with her. "I didn't get a chance to write back before the accident."

He glanced across the truck and smiled. *Damn those dimples.* "It's okay. I'm glad you're home even though the circumstances aren't the best."

I need to just tell him I haven't read his letter instead of making it sound like I know what the hell he's talking about.

"Wayne, listen. I…"

"It's fine, darlin'," he said, taking her hand and kissing her fingers. "We'll work it out once you're better."

Better? She'd never get better unless she let them amputate according to her doctors in Washington, D.C., but she didn't know if she could go through with the surgery. What would Wayne say? Would he still find her attractive once she only had half of one leg? She didn't think so.

"There's something I have to decide on while I'm home. I don't know if I can."

"I'll be there for you. I hope you know that."

"Really?"

"Of course." They pulled up in front of her parent's ranch and he shut the truck off. "Talking. Make it a priority, okay? We need to get some things out in the open." He jumped out, grabbed the chair, then opened the door. "What do you want me to do? I don't want to step on your toes anymore, babe. I know how independent you are."

"If you grab my crutches, then help me into the chair that would be great."

"Anything you say, darlin'."

Surely he's kidding. Wayne Ridges kissing her ass? Who'da thought.

Within seconds, he'd scooped her up and put her in the chair. "You need to quit lugging me around like this, Wayne. You'll hurt yourself."

"Babe, I wrestle thousand pound bulls for a livin'. One little bit like you ain't gonna hurt me. I could lift you and the chair without hurtin' nothin'. Now, be quiet so I can take care of you for a minute or two. I kinda like this part."

Shit! Seriously?

"You're home!" her mother yelled from the porch as she jogged down the stairs. "Maggie MacPherson. You look a mess, honey." Her mother's hands were going a mile a minute as she talked. "Get her up on the porch, Wayne. She needs to get out of the sun."

"I'm fine, Mom."

"You are not. You've been shot in the leg. You need to recuperate, not be outside in this heat."

"Shot? I knew you'd been hurt pretty badly, but not about the bullet wound," Wayne added, his eyes wide. "You aren't going back there, are you?"

"No. I've been discharged because of my injury. It's serious, Wayne. I won't gain mobility back in my knee at all. I can't do my job with this damage."

"You're alive. That's the most important thing."

"Can we talk about this later? I really need to change the dressing on this and rest."

"Of course you do, Maggie," her mother said, directing them up onto the porch and through the front door. "I'll get the stuff to clean it with if you'll take her into the guest room down here. She won't be able to do stairs so I've made up the room off your dad's office."

"Thanks, Mom."

"Of course, Mrs. MacPherson."

"You know better, Wayne Ridges. I'm Alice to you. Not Mrs. MacPherson."

"Hard habits to break, ma'am."

"Well if you are going to be hanging around my Maggie, you'll be family in no time, so call me Alice."

"All right, ma'am."

She rolled her eyes and looked at the ceiling. "Men," Alice mumbled as she headed for the kitchen.

"Okay, up you go," he said, picking her up in his arms again. "Don't say a word. I like holding you like this."

"Fine, but I think you're taking advantage of the situation."

He laughed and headed down the hall. "Of course, I am." Once he reached the bedroom, he kicked the door shut behind them before placing her on the bed. "Need me to help you with your pants?"

"I can get them, thanks."

"You aren't helping my cause here much, Maggie mine."

"You'll have to fill me in on what your cause is, Wayne, because I'm lost."

"You back in my bed however I can get you." He skimmed his fingers down her cheek before cupping her jaw with his hand.

"You don't understand. I'm not the same person I was back in Vegas. I've seen things, done things and been around things that would make a sane person cringe. Bodies mutilated beyond recognition. Bullets flying. People dying. Bombs exploding. I can't even sleep the whole night these days without waking up in a cold sweat." Perspiration broke out on her forehead. Her pulse jumped to a steady, rapid thumping in her chest.

"I can handle it."

"I can't." She pulled away from his touch. "Don't you see? I'm different. We're different."

"I don't see how, Maggie. We were great together in Vegas."

"Vegas seems like so long ago," she whispered, dropping her gaze to the floor. "I feel old and worn out, Wayne."

"You're only twenty-three."

"War does that to a person. You can't understand."

"Let me try. Tell me."

She licked her lips, and then blew out a calming breath. Her heart rate slowed as the anxiety of the situation slowly drained out of her. "Being buried in a bunker with snipers trying to mow you down with every movement is terrifying. Watching the guy next to you die and knowing there isn't anything you can do about it. Those things change a person."

"I thought you were working on planes."

"I do, but we are all basically grunts when the time comes. I had to carry around a weapon at all times because we never knew when someone might try to shoot at us. Some of the people over there loved us, but many others hated everyone not Muslim. The blowing dust. The heat. It isn't like Texas heat. The grit gets into everything. You have to constantly clean your weapon to try to keep the dirt from jamming it."

He enveloped her hands in his, stroking his thumb over her knuckles.

Tears rolled down her cheeks. "The day I got shot, I'd just finished my shift after welding all day. I wanted nothing more than a hot shower, some food and to read your letter."

A moment later, he brushed the wetness from her face. "It'll be okay."

"No!" She pulled her hands from his grasp and pushed at his chest. "Don't you see? I'm not the same girl who fucked you six months ago. I'm not!"

"Yes, you are. I know you've changed a bit, but deep down inside, you are still Maggie MacPherson. Maggie mine."

"I never got a chance to read your letter. I'm not even sure where the envelope is."

"Let me grab your duffle from the truck. Maybe it's in there." Within moments, he'd returned with her duffle in hand, sitting the bulky round bag down at her feet. She leaned over and unlocked the combo lock as she bit her lip. *Why did he want me to read this letter so badly? What's written on the pages? Goodbye? If so, why is he still here?*

He pulled out several of her uniform pants, shirts and other miscellaneous items. Her cut BDU shirt lay at the bottom of the bag. "Is this the one you were wearing?"

"I assume so since the material is cut. I'm surprised they saved it. I figured they would have tossed it into the garbage."

The Call of Duty

The crinkle of paper brought a smile to her mouth. Maybe the letter made it through everything. *God, I hope so.*

Wayne reached into the front left pocket and withdrew the envelope.

"It made it!" She reached for the letter, but he held the envelope out of her reach. "I thought you wanted me to read it?"

"I do. I want to tell you something first before you read this."

"What?"

"This letter was written several weeks ago. I started the thing right after I left you in Vegas."

"You did?"

"Yeah. It took me several tries to write the blasted thing before I sent it off."

"But you sent two before I got this one."

"Yeah, I did. Those were easy to write. They had basic things like the goings on here in Shipley. My parents. The ranch. My siblings. Nothing major. No emotions. Just things."

"And this one?"

"Read it."

She opened the envelope and slowly drew out the paper, unfolding it and straightening out the wrinkles so she could read his expressive scrawl.

> *Dear Maggie,*
> *This is so hard for me to write. You can't even imagine.*
>
> *Spending the last two weeks with you here in Vegas has been so special to me. You've given me something I never thought I would find, acceptance and love.*
>
> *You never knew it, but I found you so sweet in high school, I couldn't ask you out. At sixteen there is only one thing on a guy's mind...sex. I couldn't spoil you like that, so I went out with the girls who would give it up.*

> *Finding you in Vegas seemed like fate to me. You have no idea how nervous I was trying to figure out how to get you in my bed after we met at the bar. My riding buddies thought it was funny as hell. True, I usually don't have a problem getting girls to go to bed with me, but you meant more to me than a quick tumble between the sheets. I couldn't tell you then because you wanted to keep things simple.*

Tears welled up in her eyes and fell down her cheeks. She glanced up at Wayne, but his features began to blur with her tears.

> *I should have told you before you left, but I thought you wouldn't believe me. Really, how does someone fall in love in two weeks? I did though. Yes, I love you, Maggie mine, and I hope to God he keeps you safe while you are in that hellhole. I need you to come back to me.*

Shivers rolled down her arms. He loved her?

> *Please stay safe and write when you can. Hold my love close to your heart and know you mean the world to me. I can't wait for you to come home so I can tell you all this in person.*

> *Love, Wayne*

"You love me?"

A big grin spread across his face as he nodded. "How could I not? You've been in my thoughts constantly since I found you in the bar in Vegas. You've become my life, Maggie." He raked his fingers through his hair. "When I heard you got hurt, I almost went out of my mind. You can ask your mom. I drove her nuts until I heard you would be all right. I couldn't sleep. I couldn't eat. My parents were worried I would drive myself to Washington to check on you when I heard they'd transferred you to Walter Reed."

She laughed through her tears.

"I never thought I'd ever fall in love with anyone, but you bulldozed your way into my heart. I haven't been able to think of anything expect you in months."

"I love you too, Wayne."

"Thank God!" He grabbed her and pulled her into his lap. "I was so afraid you couldn't see past the playboy bullrider, to the man underneath."

"I always knew there was more to you than what the media portrayed you as."

"Don't get me wrong. I did most of what they said, but it's all behind me. I'm committed to you and only you."

Frowning, she wiggled her way out of his lap.

"What's wrong?"

"There is something you need to know, Wayne. I have a hard decision to make about my body and I'm afraid it will affect how you feel about me. Not only do I have PTSD but I won't ever have full mobility in my leg again. I'll be a cripple for the rest of my life."

"First, what is PTSD?"

"Post Traumatic Stress Disorder. It's the reason I wake up screaming some nights or sweating enough to drench the sheets."

"I'll hold you through your nightmares."

"It's more than that, Wayne. Sometimes I wake up and I don't know where I am. I could hurt you."

He laughed and tried to pull her close again.

"I'm serious! I've been trained to hurt people in combat situations. If I'm not aware of what's going on, I could seriously hurt you."

"Come on, Maggie. I'm a guy."

"Fine. Stand up." She grabbed the crutches he'd brought from the truck so she could stand in front of him. "Take a punch at me."

"I'm not going to hit you."

"Do like I said. You won't hit me."

He rolled his eyes, but pulled back his arm. His punch came at her fast and furious. She grabbed his wrist, twisted his arm until she almost popped the shoulder out of the socket, which dropped him to his knees.

"Okay. I get it."

"Did I hurt you? I'm sorry."

"No, it's fine, darlin'. I understand now," he said, gingerly coming to his feet.

"I need counseling, which I plan to get now, since I will be discharged due to my injury."

"Good. I hope someone can help you get through these nightmares."

"It should help."

"What's the other thing you were talking about?"

She bit her lip.

"Maggie?"

After a moment, she struggled to sit back on the bed. How did she tell him she wouldn't be a whole woman anymore? Losing a leg meant her whole life would change. She'd be an amputee. Half a person. In constant pain.

"The doctors want me to amputate my leg above the knee, Wayne. The damage is extensive. I only have a week or so to decide."

"So we get another opinion. They're always makin' strides in working with people who have bad injuries, right?"

She shook her head. "I've already talked to the top doctors in the field. There isn't anything they can do. The nerve damage alone is bad. I can't feel my foot."

"I love you, Maggie. It doesn't matter if you only have one foot."

"I'll be a damned cripple, Wayne. Don't you see?"

"I'm not in love with your foot." He dropped to his knees, kissing her damaged foot. "I'm not in love with your leg." The kisses continued to trail up her leg until he reached her bandaged knee. "I am in love with your pussy." She giggled. "I'm in love with you. All of you whether it's damaged or not. Maggie MacPherson is what I need and what I want whether you have two feet or not." He reached up and kissed her on the mouth. "But you have to come to terms with your injuries. It would be no different than if I got hurt badly on a bull."

"It wouldn't matter to me."

"Yet you think your injury would matter to me?"

"It's different."

"Why?"

"You'd be injured doing something you love. Bull riding is your life."

"And the military was yours until recently. Whether you have two feet or one foot, I love you. All of you, but especially the pussy."

"You're bad."

"Just telling you the truth. I can't wait to be buried deep there again. I hope it is soon because I feel like I'm about to explode."

She glanced up at him through her lashes. "I could help you with your problem, you know. I'm pretty good with my mouth." A soft knock on the door interrupted their dirty conversation. "Come in."

"I brought the bandages. I thought I'd give you two a little time to talk."

"Thanks, Mom. It meant a lot."

"So did you tell her?" she asked, glancing at Wayne with an expected look.

"Tell her what?"

"Oh good grief, Wayne. If you aren't in love with her, I don't know what love looks like. I hope you finally told her."

"It's a good thing too, Mom, because I love him too."

"I'm so glad. You two look good together."

"But I have a decision to make and I think it will make things change between us, but Wayne doesn't think so."

"Oh?"

"They want me to amputate my leg."

Chapter Three

"Amputate?" Her mother dropped into the chair near the window. "As in cut it off. Why? I thought your wound was healing?"

"There is massive nerve damage. I can't feel my foot and the tissue is dying because lack of blood flow. The damage to the major artery can't be repaired. Neither can the issues with the nerves. They have to amputate."

"I keep telling her it doesn't matter to me, but she won't listen."

"We shall see after it's done how you feel. You might be totally grossed out."

Wayne sighed and rolled his eyes. "Do you want me to help you change the bandage?"

"I can do it."

"I want to help. I need to show you blood and stuff doesn't gross me out. I've seen enough injuries with the guys I ride with, it doesn't bother me anymore."

"Good, because blood makes me ill, especially if it's my own."

"Let me help you with your pants," he said, waggling his eyebrows.

She rolled her eyes and shook her head. "You just want in my pants."

"I think I'll leave you two alone for now. Wayne can help you with the bandages. I'll get dinner ready."

She stood on her wobbly foot while he dropped to his knees in front of her to work her pants down her legs. "I kind of like you in this position."

"Are you hot for me?" he asked, tossing her pants over his shoulder. "I can smell you."

"You don't have to do anything to make me hot for you."

Two fingers inched under the elastic of her underwear. She shivered with need to have him touch her. "Touch me. It's been too damned long." Once she eased back on the bed, she spread her thighs to give him access.

"We can't do anything with your mom in the other room." His nose nudged her mound. "You smell like heaven. My cock is hard as a rock right now. Besides, I don't want to rush things after so long. I'll explode the minute I get inside you."

"Help me change the bandage first. We'll go from there afterward."

He grabbed the scissors her mom left on the bed along with the rolls of gauze and cut the dirty bandages away. After he slowly peeled the dressing off, she laid back on the bed so she couldn't see the shredded flesh. What would he think? Did it gross him out to see her knee in all its gory details?

"It's not even bloody, Maggie."

"No? I haven't seen the area since it happened."

"They stitched everything up. It's just a wound, babe. Nothing bloody or yucky about it."

She pushed up on her elbows and glanced down. He was right. She had several stitches in the skin but nothing hanging out or tissue flapping in the breeze. "Oh. I thought it would be gross."

Using the warm washcloth her mother brought up, he washed the area around the stitches before he dried them off. "Does it hurt?"

"Not really. I can't feel anything from my thigh down."

"I'm sorry, babe."

"There isn't anything for you to be sorry for."

"You shouldn't have been over there in the first place. Where were the damned guards? Weren't they supposed to be watching for shit like this?"

"I had to, Wayne. Being there came with the job I signed up to do. I'm a casualty of the war."

He gripped her shoulders in his hands. "You aren't a casualty. You're alive and well."

"I'm not well. I'm sick. The PTSD took care of that. I'm about to lose half my damned leg. You don't get it. I'm not a whole person anymore. I'm split into tiny bits and pieces. I don't think I'll ever be whole again."

He grabbed her in a fierce hug. "I'll help you get well again, Maggie. I love you."

"I love you too, Wayne, but I think I'm beyond what your love can do for me. I think you should go."

"Don't send me away. We can work through this."

"Until I get the amputation and work with a counselor, we can't work through this. It's me, not you." She laughed ruefully. "Isn't that a clique from hell."

"This isn't over," he said, climbing to his feet.

"It is for now. I have too much to get past before anything can come of a relationship between us."

He glanced back one last time before he slipped out the door, shutting it behind him. The silence of the room enveloped her in sadness. She needed him with every beat of her heart, but for some ungodly reason, she kept pushing him away. "I have to work through this stuff. I can't expect him to take on someone who is so broken. It's not fair to him."

That's total bullshit and you know it.

A quick look at her wound told her she probably didn't need the bandage anymore since the stitches were dry. She slipped on the sweat pants she found in the pile of clothes Wayne had dug out of her duffle and struggled to her feet. It sucked trying to walk without feeling in your foot, but she had to try. Leaving everything up to someone else wasn't her style and she wasn't about to start now. Crutches sucked. No doubt about it. Her underarms felt the pressure from the constant rubbing of the pads. The chafing irritated badly.

She reached for the door handle just as the door swung back open, almost knocking her to her butt.

Wayne rushed in, grabbing her by the shoulders to steady her so she didn't fall. "I'm not leaving here. I refuse to let you cut me out of your life because you're scared. Get over yourself, Maggie. This isn't only about you. You are playing with my life here too. I'm in this for the long haul."

"But what about my dreams and losing my leg?"

"It doesn't matter. Can't you get that through your thick skull? I love you and you love me. We're in this together."

"Are you two coming in for dinner?" her mother called from the dining room.

"We'll be right there, Mom." She glanced up into his intense blue eyes. Expecting to find anger, she wasn't prepared for the love shining in his gaze. "I'm sorry. I shouldn't push you away. It's not fair to you."

"No, it's not. I love you." He wrapped her in a hug, pulling her tight against his chest. "Whatever hell you're going through, I'm there too, babe. I need you. I love you. We'll do this thing together. I'll be by your side for everything. The nightmares. The learning to walk with a prosthetic. Taking care of our babies."

"Babies?"

"Of course. Loving me comes with the hazards of little feet, crying at midnight and dirty diapers, lots of them."

"That almost sounds like a proposal, Wayne Ridges."

"Well, not exactly."

"Not exactly?"

"I'm planning on a nice romantic proposal, so save your answer." He grabbed her behind the knees before he scooped her up in his arms. "Let's get some dinner and we'll go from there. I already told your parents and mine I'm staying here until you kick me out."

"My parents were okay with you being here with me in my room?"

"I told them we were getting married when I was with your mom earlier, so sshh. Don't say anything to the contrary and we'll be fine."

She giggled and buried her nose in his shoulder. "You are so sneaky."

A quick swipe of her tongue along the corded muscles of his neck had him moaning softly. "Knock it off or we won't be making an appearance at dinner."

"Would that be a bad thing?"

"Since your mother is now expecting us in the dining room shortly, I'd say yes."

* * * *

Four hours later, she snuggled up to his chest breathing in the scent uniquely Wayne, while they settled beneath the covers of her bed. The subtle mixture of man, musk with a tang of sweat clung to his skin. "You smell good."

"I didn't think we were ever going to get away from your parents."

"I can't believe my mom is planning a bridal shower already." She punched him in the side. "This is all your fault, you know."

"My fault?"

"Yes, you had to go ahead and tell them we are getting married yet you haven't really asked nor I haven't said yes."

"You are going to say yes, right?"

"Of course I am. I'm not letting my lifelong fantasy man get away from me after he's already professed his love."

His fingers danced over her shoulder and down her arm.

"Fantasy man, huh?"

"Yes. While you were off dating and fucking every girl in high school, I sat at home waiting for you to see me as a girl you could go out with." She ran her hand over the muscles of his chest. "I know you said you didn't want to spoil sweet little me, but man, I would have loved to feel all these muscles long before now."

"I didn't have all these muscles back then."

"No, but you were still hot."

"Oh yeah?"

"Please. Don't tell me you didn't see seventy-five percent of the female population of our high school panting after you in the halls?"

"Only seventy-five? I thought it was more like ninety-five." She grabbed a few tuffs of hair and pulled. "Ouch!"

"Don't get cocky, buddy."

He quickly rolled her onto her back. Her nipples stood up, begging for his mouth.

"Do you want somethin', darlin'?"

"Your mouth."

"Where?"

"On my nipple. God, please Wayne. I haven't been with anyone since we fucked in Vegas."

"Me either, babe."

His lips closed over her nipple as a heavy sigh left her lips. The slight pull of his mouth drove her need skyward. "Yes. Perfect. Bite me." He gently bit down on her extended nub. Her pussy wept. Her skin tingled. Her pussy throbbed with every beat of her heart. "Wayne, please."

He parted her legs with his knee, settling himself between her thighs. "Are you ready for me?"

"I've been ready since the moment we parted in Vegas."

His cock nudged at her opening before he gently slid home.

"I don't want soft, Wayne. Fuck me hard."

"You asked for it," he said, rising up on his hands and shoving his cock so deep, it almost hurt. The slight twinge of pain brought her need higher.

He slammed his cock into her as her pussy clasped him tighter.

"Fuck yes."

"Yes. Harder, please."

The headboard rocked against the wall as she fought a giggle in her throat. What would her parents say in the morning when they heard the noise coming from her room? She didn't think they'd care. After all, they were getting married.

Chapter Four

One month later

"Open your eyes, beautiful," Wayne whispered softly against her ear. "The doctor said you need to wake up now."

"I want to sleep. Leave me alone."

"Nope. Open those gorgeous eyes for me."

She slowly opened her eyes to see her parents, Wayne's parents and Wayne surrounding her bed. The surgery was over.

"How do you feel?"

"Groggy."

"I can imagine."

She didn't feel any different. Of course, how could she, she hadn't been able to feel her leg since the accident anyway. "Is it gone?"

"You're leg?"

She nodded as a tear slipped from the corner of her eye.

"Yes." He took her hand in his and brought it to his mouth. "Don't think about it. They'll fit the prosthetic in a few weeks and you'll be up walking in no time."

"I'm okay. I knew this day had to come sooner or later."

"Are you sure?"

"If you can still say you love me, everything will be fine."

"I love you, Maggie mine, more than life itself."

"I love you too, Wayne. God, I love you so much."

He wiped the tears from her eyes with the sheet. "No more tears."

A small giggle left her lips. "Who ever thought plain old Maggie MacPherson would wrap *the* Wayne Ridges around her little finger and have him changing diapers in nine months."

"What? Wait a minute. Nine months?"

She cringed and nodded. "You work fast Mr. Ridges."

Both sets of parents laughed as big grins spread across their faces. "We'll have to move up the wedding."

"He hasn't even asked me yet!" Maggie laughed. "Do you see a ring?"

"But he said…"

"I know what he said, Mom, but I don't even have a ring yet."

Seconds later, Wayne pulled out a small blue box. "I wanted this to be a romantic thing, but since there's now going to be a baby on the way, we'd better move this up a bit. Will you marry me, Maggie?"

She tapped her fingers against her lips. "I don't know. I mean, I should think about this for a bit. Really I…*ack*!" Wayne tickled her until she squealed, "All right! Yes, I'll marry you just as soon as we can arrange a small wedding. I don't want a huge deal. Just family."

"How about next weekend?"

"Next weekend?"

"Sure. If it's just family, we don't need invitations or anything. We can just call everyone and invite them over. We can have a barbeque behind your parent's place."

"But I can't even shop for a dress! I want to be able to stand at the altar with you so we'll have to postpone it until I have my prosthesis."

"All right. How long?"

"Six months. I need that long to get a dress and figure out how to walk on my peg leg. Of course by then I'll be huge." She twisted her mouth up and looked at the ceiling for a moment. "How about three months?"

"Three months from today."

Epilogue

"Wayne, get the baby would you please?" Maggie asked, rolling over in the bed and burying her face in the pillow. Midnight feedings sucked.

"Sure, babe, but I think you'll need to take care of her. She's probably hungry. I can't do that part."

"Grr." He laughed and bounced out of the bed. "Pigheaded man. Way too jovial for the middle of the damned night."

She smiled to herself as she heard him softly singing to their little Jenna. Really, she was the perfect baby from the time she came home. She didn't cry much except when she got hungry or needed a diaper change. He did well taking on the diaper changes and what he could do for her, but the breastfeeding made it difficult for him to do anything in the feeding department.

"Here you go, Momma."

Maggie shoved her hair out of her eyes and propped herself up on the pillows. "How's my girl?"

"Dry and hungry."

Wayne watched as she opened her gown, bringing the baby to her breast. "I love watching you feed her."

"You should go back to sleep. You have to get on the road tomorrow early to get to Cheyenne in time for the ride."

"I'm fine. I'll be there in plenty of time."

"I don't want you falling asleep at the wheel. We need you to come home safe."

He leaned over and kissed her. "I love you, Maggie."

"I love you too."

"How soon do you want to have another one?"

"Excuse me? Can we get this one out of diapers before we think of more?"

"Just asking, babe. I want a big family."

She laughed and shook her head. "I'm not popping kids out one right after the other, mister, so keep your dick in your pants. I'm not going off my birth control anytime soon."

"What would you say if I told you I wanted to retire?"

His admission startled her. Never in a million years would she have thought of Wayne retiring right now. "If you want to, Wayne. It's up to you. It's your career."

"I know, but I'm on top right now. I'd rather go out in a number one position than retire a broken shell of my former self."

"I love you and will support you in anything you do just like you support me with my nightmares. I will hold you through the rough days because I know there will be some when you second-guess quitting."

"It's settled then. After this season, I'm done. I'll be home full time taking care of this place and raising our babies with you."

"I'm glad. You're my life. I wouldn't want you any other way."

THE END

SERVING HER HEART
D. F. Krieger
Copyright © 2012

Chapter One

Laurie inwardly groaned as she clutched the cell phone to her ear and attempted to navigate the interstate. The voice on the other end nattered on and on without, it seemed, pausing for a breath. After five minutes straight of listening to the voice speak, Laurie issued an irritated sigh.

"Look, I know, Mom. I know you are already fifty with no grandkids, but my job doesn't give me time to find anyone and settle down. Besides, how fair would it be to any kids I did have? What am I suppose to tell them? 'I'm sorry I can't be home for Christmas or any other holiday, but being a soldier comes first'?" The silence on the other end made her grit her teeth.

It was like this every time she called her mom, especially when holidays were coming up. The subject of her lack of a husband and children were brought up and tossed at her like rotten tomatoes at a bad play. Three years now she'd been in the Army, and every single conversation eventually led to this.

"Mom, you know I love you. Don't take it personally but…chill out. You are perfectly healthy and you aren't going to die tomorrow, so quit."

The gasp on the other end of the phone made Laurie smile. "What would your father think if he heard you being this mouthy? I don't know why you had to grow up and go play soldier anyway. What about us? We miss you on the holidays."

"So adding a husband and kids to the mix who would miss me too will just make everything better, won't it?" Laurie switched the phone from one hand to the other so she could change lanes. "Mom, I'm entering a really rural area where signal dodges in and out. I'm going to get off here so I can put the pedal to the metal and get home."

"I don't see why we have to celebrate Thanksgiving two weeks early," her mother said, the tone indignant.

"You don't, but this is the only chance I had for leave. You know that people grabbed up the holiday leave like crazy since we got back from deployment last week. What do you want me to do about it? You could just do nothing this week and celebrate Thanksgiving during your normal time." She tried to keep the sarcasm and bitterness from her tone.

Her mother remained silent for so long that Laurie checked her phone to make sure they hadn't lost connection. Finally, just as she was about to call her mother's name, her mother said, "Drive safe. I love you."

"Love you too, Mom. See ya in about three more hours." She pushed a button to end the call and dropped the phone in her lap.

Three more hours until she got to fight like this with her mother in person. The whole situation stank and she hated it. Holidays or visits weren't supposed to be like this. They were *supposed* to be times of happiness and celebration. It was getting to the point that Laurie didn't even want to talk to her mother anymore.

She hated to admit it, but the deployment had almost been refreshing. Her mother wasn't the most techno-savvy person in the world, so their communication by e-mail had been far and few between. That meant less conversations that involved her mother lecturing her that she needed to find a man, settle down, have kids. In essence, live the white picket fence dream.

Laurie knew she'd never been headed for those kinds of dreams. It just wasn't her. While other girls were into cheerleading or pageants, Laurie had been playing paintball with her guy friends and fixing up old cars. Classic cars had always been a soft spot of hers, just like the vehicle she was driving now. The '78 Monte Carlo, with its curves that flared over the rear tires and loudly purring engine, was her most recent project. She'd finally had a new engine dropped in it just last week in preparation for this trip.

Just as she trailed her fingertips across the steering wheel in a gentle caress, the car jerked. The Monte Carlo began fishtailing and the wheel tugged this way and that in her hands. With all of her strength, Laurie clenched the wheel in her fists and let off the gas. She slowly guided the car to the shoulder of the interstate as she performed a constant check for vehicles around her. Thankfully, the only other car in sight was far ahead of her.

C'mon, baby. What's wrong with you? This is not the time or place. We're out in the middle of nowhere!

Once she had the car safely parked, she killed the engine and sat for a moment, catching her breath. With an older car like this, anything could be wrong, but she was betting she already knew what happened. With dread, she got out of the car and walked around to the rear.

"Ah, hell," she muttered as she eyed the obvious blown-out tire. "This sucks. I don't even have a freaking spare."

Laurie pulled out her cell and glanced at the time. It was already seven at night. Even if she managed to get a tow to the nearest mechanic shop, none of them would be open at this time of night. She didn't even bother checking for a spare. The donut tire she had wouldn't get her all the way to her parent's house. Her standby had enough life left in it to get her to the nearest town, and that was about it. She'd been meaning to put all new tires and a spare on the car, but she hadn't been home long enough to get everything done that she'd wanted to do.

I should have done it when I had the new engine put it. Who am I kidding? I didn't have the money for both. It had taken all of the money I saved from deployment just to buy that engine, pay for the Monte's storage, and have a mechanic tow and put the engine in. I was dead broke until this morning.

There was nothing left to do but call for help. Laurie got back in her driver's seat, opened up her glove box, and pulled out her insurance card. She silently thanked the higher powers that she'd had enough common sense to put roadside assistance on her insurance package. After a few moments, she had an agent on the line and was explaining her situation. Three holds and twenty minutes later, she was informed a tow truck was on its way.

She leaned her forehead against the steering wheel and let out a soft groan. "I do not want to call Mom."

Chapter Two

The thick veil of night had settled over the highway. She kept a constant eye on her rearview mirror, waiting for the tow truck to show up. Every time a vehicle sped by, it rocked the car, making her grit her teeth and clutch the wheel.

So help me, if any of them clip my car I swear I'll lose it on them! And where the hell is that mechanic?

Traffic was few and far between, which made every set of headlights cause her heart to do a two-step. *Was this vehicle the one? No, its headlights were too low to the ground, indicating it was a car. Was that one it? No, it was too big and going much too fast, definitely a semi.*

Finally, after an hour of waiting, a flashing orange set of hazards appeared in her mirror. To be on the safe side, Laurie waited until the truck pulled up directly behind her before she let herself sag in relief. The phone call to her mother had put her already frazzled nerves back on edge.

She stepped out of her car and stood beside the still-intact rear tire as she waited for the mechanic to get out. The flash of his lights caused her to raise a hand in an attempt to shield her eyes. The air was cooling off rapidly, nipping at her bare arms. She hadn't brought a jacket despite the fact it was fall. She'd packed with expectations to be at her parents' in less than three hours.

When the driver got out, it took a moment for her to really see him. Laurie didn't know what she had been expecting, but it certainly wasn't what landed out of the high-set wrecker, that was for sure. The closer the mechanic got, the more she wanted to curl up in a ball, hide, and stare at him.

He's freaking gorgeous!

The mechanic had pale blond hair, stood about six feet tall, and looked like a golden god from some ancient fairy tale. As he approached her, he extended his hand in greeting.

"Evening, ma'am. Do you happen to know what's wrong? The company that called me to come get you only said you needed a tow, they never said why."

Oh my goodness, that southern drawl is to die for! Usually Laurie didn't care for southern accents, she attributed them to morons and uneducated jerks, but with this man it made her think of home-style cooking, tire swings on a sunny summer afternoon, and... *No, don't go there. You've been listening to your mom gripe too much. Leave it. Guys like him are either already married, gay, or too good to get involved with a girl who's always gone.*

"Rear passenger tire blew," she managed to say as she shook his hand. The raspy sound of her own voice made her wince. Laurie tried very hard not to let her inner gearhead squee over the rough calluses she felt on his palm.

The man, Patrick if she were to trust the embroidered name on his shirt, nodded before walking around the car to check it out. "Do you need me to change the tire?"

She shook her head at his question, then walked closer when she realized he probably couldn't see her that well from the other side of the car in the dark. "No. All I have is a donut and that won't get me where I need to go. I need a tow and new tires."

Patrick pointed at the cab of his truck. "Get on in and buckle up. I'll pull around to the front of your car and load her up. I gotta tell ya though, this late at night, there won't be a mechanic open to slap new tires on it for you."

Laurie tried not to let the mixed emotions show on her face. Part of her was relieved that she wouldn't have to see her family tonight, the other part was worried. "I guess I can stay at a hotel for the night. What time will the mechanic open in the morning?"

The tow truck driver shook his head as he walked around and opened the cab door for her. "You look like you're freezing. Get on in. And, uh, everybody is closed for the weekend. There won't be a single mechanic open 'til Monday morning."

She froze mid-step, and turned her head to stare at him. "Monday? I don't have until Monday."

"I'm sorry, ma'am." To his credit, Patrick's face did show some honest sympathy. "Let's get your car loaded up and we'll get you to town."

Laurie nodded, but her stomach didn't agree with this situation, not a single.bit. Her leave expired on Wednesday. If the mechanic didn't open until Monday morning, she wouldn't be getting to her parent's house until around noon, at least. All the family they had invited would be long gone, returned to their jobs and their own hometowns. The entire get-together her mother had arranged for an early Thanksgiving would be over and done with, and Laurie was the whole reason they were having it this early. Guilt ate at her like a rat with sharp teeth.

When Patrick got in, she kept her mouth shut. All she wanted to do was whine, beg and plead with him to help her find some mechanic to bully into fixing her tires. Anyone who would take pity on her and slap at least one tire on. Instead, she stared straight out the windshield.

As if sensing her distress, the mechanic kept his peace. From the corner of her eye, she noticed he kept glancing at her every little bit. He'd open his mouth slightly, as if he was going to say something, then close it again.

It didn't take long for him to maneuver the truck around to the front of her Monte Carlo. Just before Patrick got out, he said, "Be back in just a moment. Stay put and warm up, ma'am."

Laurie shot him a half-smile acknowledging his words, but didn't attempt to reply. The strong sexy scent of his cologne, a deep spicy musk, made her want to bury her face in his chest and inhale deeply. The smell forced a whole new train of thought to fight with the ugly one already dominating her head.

Mom's going to be so pissed at me.

Damn that man is cute.

I don't even want to call her and let her know about all this. I'm going to put off calling her until tomorrow.

Wouldn't mind spending a weekend with this guy though.

Pictures of her kissing him, touching him, making him smile up at her while he lay underneath her kept filling her mind. The loud sound of the driver's door being opened almost scared her out of her skin.

"Whoa, sorry." He offered her an apologetic smile. "Next time should I knock first? That way I don't scare you."

"Oh, no, I..." She knew she was blushing. The burn of her embarrassment made her cheeks feel like they were on fire. "I guess I've just got a lot on my mind," she finished lamely.

"I bet you do. I imagine it's hard to be in a situation like this, all alone. Is your husband deployed?" Patrick pushed her suitcase into the niche behind his seat, pulled himself into the cab and shut the door.

"P-pardon me? My husband?" Laurie couldn't help but stare at him in surprise. Where on earth had he gotten the idea she was married?

"Yeah." The mechanic pointed at his own chest, around sternum height. "I saw the dog tags. I assumed that means he's military and, since he's not here, that he's gone on deployment."

"Oh!" Laurie burst out laughing, relieved that the misunderstanding was over something so simple. "No, no. No husband."

"Boyfriend?"

With a shake of her head she replied, "Nope, no boyfriend or husband in my life at all. Me. I'm in the military."

"I don't suppose you want some lengthy sermon about how I appreciate your service?"

Laurie snickered, then shook her head again. "No, those tend to irritate me. Those and the lectures where people tell me the battlefield isn't a woman's place, like we're still in the 1700's or something."

He laughed and she found herself melting on the spot. The sound was deep, genuine, and she got the feeling he didn't laugh often. It made her want to tell lame jokes in an attempt to illicit the sound from him again. The rest of the drive they made small talk, and the more she heard him speak, the more she wanted him to keep doing it. By the end of the thirty-minute drive, she'd finally convinced him to call her by her name instead of ma'am. When they pulled into town, Patrick took an exit off the interstate and pulled into a hotel parking lot.

"The mechanic shop I'll be dropping your car off at is just down the block from this place. It's not the best hotel in the world, but it's clean and has good prices. They should cut you a deal since you're a break down." Patrick pulled into a spot in front of the foyer and put the tow truck in park.

"Do I want to puzzle over why you're so knowledgeable on this hotel and its cleanliness?" Laurie shot him a wry grin, hoping it conveyed the joke. She still wasn't sure if he was fluent in sarcasm.

The smile on his face reassured her immediately. "We get lots of break downs and, seeing as how I'm one of two towers in this town, I'm often on call during the nights. Though, when I pick up pretty women who've broken down all alone on the highway, I like to invite myself up to their room."

Laurie laughed even as a thrill zipped its way through her body. "Oh really now? And how many of these women would you say you've rescued and seduced in such a manner."

Patrick's expression turned serious as he sat up straight and studied her. "Point five," he replied.

"Point five? What kind of number is that?" Laurie wrinkled her nose, confused by his answer.

"Well, I think I might be about halfway through my first try." He grinned at her and she could have sworn the entire cab of the truck lit up. "Now I implement my cunning strategy of blackmail."

Almost involuntarily, Laurie licked her lips. *Blackmail, eh? I hope it involves a kiss, that's for sure.* "What strategy would that be?" She was proud that she managed to keep her voice steady despite the increased heart rate she was experiencing.

"I might be able to convince the mechanic at the shop to come in tomorrow morning and fix your car up, *if...*" He paused and she waited, holding her breath. "If you were willing to go to dinner with me in about an hour."

Even though Laurie wanted to whoop her joy to the world, she managed to contain it. Instead, she leaned forward and in a seductive tone said, "What if I say no?"

"Then I convince the mechanic anyway, clean up, buy flowers, and try harder." Patrick winked at her.

"I'll see you in an hour." She opened the door, pulled her suitcase through the opening behind the seat, climbed out, and made her way to the hotel doors. The bounce in her step was almost as big as the butterflies in her stomach.

A date! I haven't been on a date since high school. Guys don't seem to really like military girls where I'm stationed at. Oh my gosh, I got a date with a gorgeous guy!

Chapter Three

Laurie paced in the foyer outside the hotel and tried not to panic. It was five minutes after their agreed upon hour mark, and Patrick still hadn't shown up. The rumble of an engine, the kind that only comes from muscle cars and fun pickup trucks, caught her attention. She paused, listening to the purr of the motor from the nearby stoplight, trying to imagine what kind of engine it was.

The familiar yearning, a combination of elation and desire, pooled in the pit of her stomach and made her vision blur. She loved old cars. She always had and knew she always would. There was just something about vintage vehicles, their look, the sound they made, that had her heart in such a way Laurie sometimes wondered if a man ever would. When she was working with classic cars she felt complete, useful, and in her element.

The engine revved and she craned her neck in hopes to catch a glimpse of the vehicle as it drove by. Instead, a thrill washed through her as it came into view, and turned into the parking lot. The car was simply gorgeous. There was no other word for it. She had difficulty seeing the color with only the streetlamps to illuminate, but the paintjob looked almost...No...It couldn't be.

The Corvette Stingray pulled up under the well lit canopy and Laurie gasped. A chameleon paintjob graced the car, causing a rainbow effect of green, gold, and purple metallic sheen to ripple before her eyes. Ever since Laurie had seen chameleon paint, she'd wanted nothing more than to have a car covered in it. The engine changed from the high sounding growl to a lower purr as the driver shifted the vehicle into park.

I wonder if Patrick would think I'm weird if I creamed myself over this car?

As if summoned by her thoughts, the car door opened and Patrick rose out of the vehicle. "She's a beauty, ain't she?"

Surprise zinged through her. How the hell was a tow truck driver able to afford something like this? "You...This car is yours?" Laurie tried desperately to keep her jealousy down.

"Chevrolet Corvette Stingray, 1972. Chameleon paint job on everything, including the frame under the hood." The pride in Patrick's voice was matched by the evident pride in his face.

"Is she yours?" Laurie ran a hesitant finger across the driver's side rearview mirror.

"Lock, stock, and barrel. Cora was my project before I was ever near getting my driver's license when I was a teenager. I knew what I wanted, and I knew I had to build her myself." Patrick walked to the passenger side and opened the door. "Much as I'd love to go on and on about my car, I'm also hungry. My lady?"

Flattered at the gesture of him opening her door, Laurie shot him a smile. As she walked around the car, she couldn't take her eyes off it. The way the paint shimmered and changed colors as she moved made her feel like she was in an altered reality. "Your car is so gorgeous," she whispered in awe.

"So is yours. Once I got that Monte Carlo to the shop, I went ahead and pushed it into the garage. That thing's a beauty. Whoever restored it knew a thing or two about cars. You must have got yourself a hell of a deal." Patrick waited for her to slide into the car, then closed her door.

When he got in on the driver's side, Laurie grinned at him mischievously. "The person who restored the Monte says thank you for the compliment."

He paused, tilted his head, and raised an eyebrow. After a moment, he shook his head and turned the key. "Nope, don't believe it."

Laurie dropped her jaw in surprise. "What do you mean you don't believe it?"

"You are too beautiful," he replied. "Everyone knows women as pretty as you don't know a thing about cars."

"Oh yeah?" Laurie could feel the ire rising in her. She glared at him, wishing her gaze was full of daggers. "I can tell you just from the sound that your car has a 350 engine in it."

The corner of Patrick's lip twitched and Laurie's anger flew out the window. He'd been *teasing* her.

Without thinking, she punched him in the arm...hard. "You jerk!"

"Ow!" He made a show of rubbing his bicep before pulling out of the parking lot. "Be gentle, lady, I'm the good guy here."

Laurie crossed her arms over her chest in indignation, but she couldn't help the smile curving her lips. "You really had me going for a moment. I was about to get so mad."

Patrick glanced at her before returning his attention to the road. "You've been given shit over it in the past, huh?"

The sobering statement caused Laurie to drop her arms and stare out the car window. "When you're a girl, who likes guy things, guys don't tend to like you. If they do, it's because they see you as one of the guys. Never date worthy. I guess...I guess it's part of the reason I joined the Army. There, I don't feel so out of place. Lots of beautiful women there, and contrary to popular belief, not many of us are lesbians either."

Silence reigned between them for quite a few moments before Patrick said, "I'm sorry."

"Don't be, it's not your fault people were mean to me when I was a kid." She reached over and placed her hand on his arm, hoping to comfort him.

When she looked back out the windshield, they were pulling into the parking lot of a restaurant. She frowned as she studied it, uncertainty clenching her stomach. The place wasn't a major food chain. In fact, the name displayed in neon letters wasn't anywhere she'd ever heard of before.

Patrick must have seen her face because he chuckled as he killed the engine and took out his keys. "Don't worry, it's a good place to eat. It's a mom and pop joint that stays open all night. I like coming here because I know it's open no matter when I get hungry. And they serve breakfast or dinner, no matter what time of day."

Laurie continued to stare a moment before getting out. In the end, she was too hungry to care what the building looked like. The gravel of the parking lot crunched under her feet as she walked, and the chill night air nipped at her arms once again. Laurie hunched in on herself as she tried to stay warm.

"Here, I grabbed this for you." Patrick handed her a long sleeve button-up dress shirt. "I didn't figure you had a coat or you'd have worn it."

Grateful, she slipped the shirt on before they walked through the door of the restaurant. She was surprised to find, when they walked in, that the interior atmosphere was nothing like she'd feared. Where she'd expected a bar with a rowdy environment and loud music, instead she found a romantic setup with quiet classical music playing and low lighting.

"Wow. Okay, I'll admit it is nicer than I expected. That leaves one question still unanswered."

"Oh?" Patrick led her to a table in the back corner and pulled out a chair for her. As she seated herself with a murmured thanks, he asked, "What's that?"

"How's the food?"

* * * *

The food, Laurie decided, was excellent. It was just the home style cooking she'd not only been craving, but needed. The only thing better than the food was the company she was keeping. Throughout dinner they had laughed, talked, and shared stories of their childhood. Every moment she spent with Patrick made her feel more and more like a normal woman.

That was dangerous.

"So where are you headed, anyway?" Patrick sipped his soft drink as he waited for her answer.

"Bingham, about three hours south of here. My parents live there." Laurie trailed a finger across her glass as she played with the condensation. "I was supposed to be visiting them for an early Thanksgiving dinner this weekend."

"Supposed to be? You make it sound like that isn't going to happen." He reached over and placed his hand on top of hers. It drew her attention back to his face.

"I have no idea if you managed to get the mechanic to agree to come in tomorrow. Even then, a part of me doesn't want to go…"

There, I said it. Laurie was surprised with herself. Surely she did want to go, right? Yet, even as she wondered, she knew deep in her heart that the answer was a resounding *No*. She was sick to death of the constant badgering from her mother and aunts about when she was going to land a man and get *a sensible lifestyle*. And, if she was being totally honest, she didn't mind the idea of being stuck here with Patrick for a couple more days.

"Why don't you want to go?" he asked. "The stories you've told me about growing up makes it sound like you have a pretty cool family."

"They are…They were." Laurie sighed as she tried to figure out how to explain. "Mom and I don't see eye to eye on my career choice."

"Oh. Well, she's probably just concerned. Mothers are supposed to be that way, y'know." He shot that lopsided grin at her that she was coming to adore. "Besides, I'd never stop you from being in the Army. If that's your thing, then I understand. But that doesn't mean I won't worry about you too."

Before Laurie could say anything or process his comment, Patrick stood up, pulled her from her seat, and pressed his mouth to hers. The kiss was electrifying and encompassed her very being. When he pulled away, they stood staring at each other, their breathing heavy.

If this is what a kiss is like with him, I can't wait to experience sex with him!

Chapter Four

A half hour later they were back at the hotel, and Laurie couldn't keep her hands off Patrick. In all honesty, it seemed the feeling was mutual. He was touching, kissing, and caressing her just as much as she was him. After all, he'd started it.

As they made their way across the room, Laurie subtly shifted her position until the back of Patrick's knees bumped into the bed. With a soft push, she smiled as he landed on the mattress. "May I join you?" The seductive purr of her voice startled her, yet she managed to maintain her poise.

"Listen I…I don't want you to think I normally do this." His vibrant blue eyes stared up at her, expressing his worries. "I don't want to go any further than this if you aren't okay with it."

"Uh…" Laurie looked around before climbing on top of him. "I'm not sure I should point this out, but it looks to me like I'm doing the forcing. Maybe I should offer you the same."

"No, no. I'm good. I'm totally okay with this."

"Good. I'd hate to think you weren't enjoying yourself." Laurie leaned forward and kissed him.

The hard rod in his blue jeans helped relieve what doubts she was having. Laurie hadn't been with a guy in years, not since her boyfriend from her senior year of high school ditched her when she announced her plans to join the Army. Since then, she'd been a little jaded. If a guy wasn't willing to stick her lifestyle out, then she didn't need anyone at all. But then Patrick came along with his sense of humor, his sexy physique, and his equal love of classic cars. He was just the right combination to be very wrong for her self-imposed restriction from one night stands.

His hands splayed across her back, and he began applying slight pressure, lifting and lowering her body. Laurie allowed herself to respond and soon, despite the clothes, they were grinding against each other while raining kisses on every available exposed and naked patch of skin.

"You're so sexy," Patrick murmured against her throat.

His words were all she needed to spur her into further action. With confidence, she sat up and took off the long sleeve dress shirt he'd lent her. Then, before she could talk herself out of it, she grasped the hem of her shirt, and pulled it over her head. His appreciative groan was reward enough for her courage.

"Laurie...I—"

She placed two fingers on Patrick's lips to silence him. "Shhh. If we talk, I'll get scared and I might run. That would suck, cause you have my car hostage, so I have nowhere to run to."

"You don't have to have sex with me to get your car fixed," he protested.

"I know. My choice to have sex with you is because I want to, because I like you. It has nothing to do with my car." She enveloped his mouth in a kiss until she felt him relax under her and become caught up once more in the moment.

Soon all coherent thought, all reason was lost to those kisses. The way his hands slid over her body, the way his tongue heated the skin of her breasts. She wasn't quite sure when her clothes came off, only that she was naked and now on her back. Patrick towered above her, his own body completely exposed for her perusal.

"Somebody works out," Laurie said as she traced a finger over his sculpted stomach.

He grinned down at her, captured her hand with his own, then placed a kiss on the fingertip. "Somebody lifts heavy car parts on a regular basis and that's the same as going to a gym."

Laurie wrapped her legs around Patrick as she urged him toward her entrance. "Give me a workout, I've been a lazy girl."

The grin on his face broadened, faltered, then disappeared. "Wait a minute. I...uh." A flush began to creep along his cheeks and neck.

Fear tightened around Laurie's heart as she stared up at him. *Ah hell, what could possibly be wrong?* "What? What is it?"

"I don't have any condoms." He ran a hand through his hair, tousling it.

The urge to laugh filled her, but she stifled it. Now was not the time. "It's okay. I'm on the shot. We're covered."

At his speculative look she grinned. "The shot keeps us girls from having our inconvenient friend so the military doesn't have to worry. It's optional, but I like the side effect enough that I stay on it even when I'm not deployed."

She could tell her explanation helped because he nodded at her words and his flush receded. "In that case..." He settled between her thighs and the tip of his dick rubbed against her entrance.

When he entered her, it was like fireworks going off. Everything around her, inside her body, and inside her mind was flipped on at once. The world itself seemed to light up. She didn't remember sex being this pleasurable before, but then again, she wasn't in the backseat of a car either.

Laurie tried to smother her moans by placing her lips against Patrick's collarbone. She didn't want people in the room next door to hear them. The more he thrust, though, the harder it was to keep that train of thought. Until Patrick, Laurie had thought the G-spot a myth, a fabrication created by women to convince themselves to keep giving sex a try. Now, as his dick pounded against a spot that flared with pleasure, she knew it truly existed...and it felt spectacular!

Their union was basic vanilla sex, and didn't last long. It didn't need to. The sexual desire that had been building since she first laid eyes on him had her well on the edge and ready for the orgasm that slammed her body within a matter of minutes. As her pussy muscles squeezed around him, milking him, Patrick groaned. His dick throbbed inside of her as he thrust hard and deep, coming.

As they lay there, panting, Laurie basked in the afterglow of her orgasm. "Wow," she finally whispered. "Can we do that again?"

Patrick lifted his head and smiled down at her. "Is that a request for an encore?"

"For sure." She swooped in and nibbled his bottom lip. "More, sir?"

"With pleasure," he replied.

* * * *

Laurie blinked as she tried to focus on the clock. A groggy mist surrounded her brain, forcing her thoughts to stay primal and to use small words. It was two o'clock in the morning, and they'd made love several times before collapsing together in an exhausted tangle of limbs and sheets.

"Patrick?"

"Mmmm?" The sound of his voice vibrated against her shoulder blades.

She smiled, yet sadness clenched her heart as she asked the next words. "This is a one night stand, right?"

"Doesn't have to be," he murmured, the slur of his words indicating he was still half-asleep.

A thrill traveled through her body and straight to her stomach. Maybe she could have a relationship after all. He'd never said if he'd managed to contact the mechanic. Perhaps she would be stuck here all weekend to develop a real relationship with him?

For the first time in a very long time, hope for a future that involved someone else filled her. Patrick had a job, he had hobbies. When she was gone, he wouldn't be bored and prone to the bad behaviors she knew some significant others pulled when their military mate was deployed. Somehow, she felt it in her very being that Patrick wouldn't do those things, wouldn't hurt her like that.

Satisfied that this weekend was turning out far better than she'd imagine, she snuggled back into the covers and went back to sleep.

Chapter Five

A knock sounded on Laurie's hotel room door, dragging her from the sleep that didn't want to release her. After a few moments, the person outside pounded on the door again.

"Housekeeping."

Laurie wanted nothing more than to beat the cheery sounding voice with a pillow. "No thank you," she called as loudly as she could.

The sound of a cart rolling down the hall was welcome music to her ears. Moments later, she heard the same cheery voice and knocking, but it was further down. With a groan, Laurie rolled onto her back and glanced over to see if Patrick had woken up.

He was gone. A quick glance around the bed revealed that his clothes were gone as well. Laurie slid out of bed and padded to the bathroom, but he wasn't there either. When she returned to the bed, she almost smacked her forehead with her palm. A piece of paper from one of those tiny hotel notepads lay on his pillow on his side of the bed. The white of the paper blended well with the pillowcase, making it almost invisible. With a shaking hand, Laurie picked it up and began to read.

> *Hey,*
> *Come to the shop when you wake up.*
> *Patrick*

A mixture of relief and distress fought within her stomach. She was happy Patrick hadn't abandoned her with some sort of message, never to be seen again. Yet, if he wanted her to come to that shop, it most likely meant the mechanic had agreed to come in and replace her tires. It was a bitter sweet situation, and wouldn't get any better unless she talked to him and made her desires known. Laurie wanted a relationship with Patrick...if he was interested.

The sooner she could ask him, the better. Hopefully he stuck around the shop to at least see her off. With that in mind, Laurie grabbed her suitcase and grabbed some fresh clothes.

* * * *

The familiar sound of power tools, with their distinctive whine, filled the air. A radio blasted 80's music in the background, though there was no chance Laurie could make out the song with the noise of the power tool overriding it. The smell of the shop relaxed her, helping her calm the anxiety that danced through her like a lizard on hot sand.

She'd worried as to whether Patrick was here until she'd walked into the parking lot. The Stingray sat next to the tow truck, its paint shining in the light as a colorful beacon of hope. The sight of the spectacular car gave her all the reassurance she needed that he wasn't gone.

The garage doors were open, allowing fresh air and light into the mechanic area. Laurie entered the building through the section her car sat in instead of using the office. She frequented these places often enough to know that going in the office would do her no good. When a mechanic was involved in a car, he did not keep an eye on the office, and she seriously doubted a receptionist or manager would be in.

A glance at the tires revealed they'd already been changed. Seeing the new set on made her aware of just how bad her old tires had been. She was lucky she'd only blown the one, and that it'd waited as long as it had. Her gaze alighted upon two legs sticking out from under her car.

"Hello?" She nudged the roller board the mechanic was laying on with her foot, worried he wouldn't be able to hear her.

The man's hands appeared as he grabbed the bottom edge of her door, and he propelled himself out. Mechanic's overalls hung loosely on his frame and, when his face appeared, Laurie's stomach performed a flip-flop.

"You? You're the mechanic?"

Patrick grinned up at her as he pulled himself to a sitting position. "Mechanic, tow truck driver, manager. You name it, I do it. I own this shop."

Laurie glanced around the inside of the building and tried to take it all in. The tools that hung against the far wall were well-used, the floor had dirt on it, but wasn't filthy. The entire shop was well-maintained and obviously used quite a bit.

"How does someone our age run a mechanic shop?" She raised an eyebrow at him.

"My dad taught me everything I know. Remember how I said he died from a heart attack about two years ago? Well, this shop was his, and I inherited. I didn't want to let it go, so I took it over. It's good money and being my own boss isn't so bad." Patrick stood and walked over to a sink where he began washing his hands. "We're one of two shops in about a seventy-five mile stretch, so business is good. The other owner and I get along since his son and I grew up together. He specializes in diesel engines, things like that, so we don't step on each other's toes."

"Wow...I'm amazed."

"You had a couple of very important bolts that were loose on your undercarriage. I decided to go through and check them all and tighten them. We don't need your transmission hitting the ground while you are driving down the interstate." Patrick grinned at her. "The tranny is pretty new, isn't it?"

Laurie blinked, surprised that a mechanic would go out of his way to ensure her safety. Immediately, she chastised herself. This was Patrick she was thinking of. If she didn't believe he could be such a good guy, then why was she willing to risk a relationship with him? "Uh, yeah. I had it installed just before I left for deployment. I tried to do it myself, but the transfer case is just so damn heavy..."

"Tell me about it! I think replacing transmissions is my least favorite job. It wouldn't be so bad if they weren't in such an awkward place," Patrick grumbled.

She stood there, staring at him. *I can talk to him. He understands me. How many people have I ever found that I could talk to like this?* "Patrick, I..." Uncertain how to continue, she started glancing around the shop.

He cleared his throat and pointed at the office. "The bill is on the desk. I know you've got a dinner to get to. Sorry I left like I did, but I knew you needed to get on the road again. I only charged half labor to help cut you a break."

"You didn't have to do that!" A flush heated her cheeks. She hadn't slept with him for special treatment and she didn't want him to think she had.

"Consider it a military discount. A thank you for going through all the shit you do to make us feel safe." He winked at her, but she could sense he'd pulled away.

She followed him into the office, feeling like a lost puppy trailing after a stranger. The situation was so awkward that she was starting to second-guess whether or not to tell him what was on her mind. What if all he'd wanted in the end was a no-strings-attached one night stand?

Silence sat heavy between them as he handed her the bill. She glanced over the invoice, pulled out her wallet, and handed him her bank card. The only noise was the sound of the card machine as he entered her information. When the receipt printed out, he offered her a smile, but the playful sparkle she'd come to know in his eyes was gone.

"Well, I guess this is it." Patrick handed her the keys to the Monte Carlo. "Don't forget to swing by the hotel and checkout. I've had clients do that before. Had a guy that even left his entire collection of suitcases, he was in such a hurry to get back on track."

"Thanks," she muttered.

She made her way to her car, her steps slow, ears straining. Her very being vibrated with hope. *Holler for me. Tell me you at least want my phone number. Ask me to stop by on my way back through when I head home. Anything, damn you!*

Laurie nearly jumped out of her skin when the cell phone in her pocket began to ring. In a quick movement, she snatched it out and looked at the caller I.D. A sinking sensation filled the pit of her stomach as she realized her mother was on the other end. *Probably calling to see where I am, how long it'll take me to get there, then nag at me as usual. If only Patrick would come.*

Then ask him, a voice urged in the back of her head. A voice made of strength and discipline and military bearing. *You are a soldier, a female soldier. You don't need to hang your hopes on a man stepping forward like some helpless little girl. Ask him yourself.*

She froze at the words, letting the truth wash over her. Laurie was a soldier, she was strong. In the past few years Laurie had done more than most people twice her age and she'd be damned if she walked away from a guy she really liked because she was too scared to ask.

"No, Patrick, this isn't it," she said, swinging around to smile at him. "At least, it doesn't have to be. If you don't have plans, I'd like you to come with me."

The look on his face was priceless. His jaw hung open, his eyes were wide, and his skin had flushed into a deep blush along his cheeks and throat.

"Are you shittin' me?"

"I'd really like it if you came with to my family's quirky ass little Thanksgiving dinner. If you can take the time away, that is." Aware of what she was asking, Laurie shifted uncomfortably. Her bravado was fading fast.

"Hell yeah, I wanna come. Let me call up the other auto shop and let him know he's got full rein." Patrick turned toward the office, then spun back around. "You sure about this? You don't have to if you do—"

"Shut up and go call that other shop before I take the keys to your Corvette hostage and make you come with." Laurie crossed her arms and glared at him.

"Ma'am, yes, ma'am!" Patrick saluted her and disappeared into the office.

Chapter Six

Laurie pulled out her cell phone and stared at it. Her mother had tried to call five times in the past ten minutes while Patrick was talking to the mechanic from the other shop. The more the phone rang, the less she wanted to talk to her. Yet, she knew her mother was just trying to figure out where she was and if she was still coming to the dinner this afternoon. With a heavy sigh, she pushed the send button and held the phone to her ear.

"I've been worried sick. Why weren't you answering your phone?" The agitation in her mother's voice immediately set Laurie on edge.

"I was paying my bill with the mechanic. I got lucky and he was nice enough to open his shop on an off day for me. I'll be heading that way in just a little bit, once I checkout of the hotel."

There was silence for a moment before her mom said, "You be careful and don't let him fuck you over. Men see a girl on the road alone and they'll either take advantage of her financially or physically."

Oh, if only you knew. She tried desperately not to giggle like a little school girl. "Mom, Patrick isn't like that. He's very nice and his price was more than reasonable."

This time the silence lasted so long that Laurie's stomach began to twist. Her mother wasn't stupid, the deliberate use of the mechanic's name made it obvious he wasn't just some dude who had fixed her car.

"I like him, Mom."

An exhale of breath made the other end of the phone crackle. "Good! Maybe he can talk you into giving up this military nonsense. Your time is almost up. We've just got a few more months to go, then you can be done and get out."

Laurie froze as she tried to control the anger her mother's words created. "Mom, I love you, but I'm going to re-up. I love being in the military and if Patrick likes me back, he'll understand."

"Don't be stupid, Laurie. Men don't sit around at home waiting for their wives to show up. He won't take the relationship seriously. You'll be someone he can screw once in awhile until he finds a girl he can really settle down with. If you're lucky he might be willing to deal with the next three months. Use your head, get out of there before you end up getting deployed again and I lose you to one of those damn bombers. Now come home, eat dinner, and we'll talk about this some more." Her mother paused for a moment before saying, "I love you."

Enough is enough. I can't take this anymore.

"Mom, I love you too, so I need you to really listen to me right now. The military isn't some phase of rebellion like you seem to think it is. The opportunities it gives me, the financial stability, and the lifestyle are all things I have come to love and depend on. If Patrick fits in with that, then he'll understand, accept me for who I am, and we'll learn to live with it. If not, he wasn't the right guy for me. Either way, I'm in no hurry to get married, nor do I have a desire currently for kids. I'm not even twenty-five yet! I have plenty of years to worry about that later. Now, I'm going to come home, I'm going to eat dinner, but I'm not going to discuss this with you anymore. I'm getting sick and tired of this lecture every time we speak." Laurie kept her tone cool despite the fact she wanted to scream.

"Laurie, honey, I—"

"No, Mom," she interrupted. "You don't understand. It's getting to the point I don't even want to talk to you or visit anymore. You keep saying you don't want to lose me, but you're pushing me away so hard that I'm about to just quit trying."

A muffled noise on the other end made her stop. It took her a few moments to realize her mother was crying. "I can't lose you! You are my only child," her mother said between sobs.

"And you're my only mother, who I love with all my heart. Being Army is hard enough. Could you try supporting me instead of spending every second of what time we do get together telling me how wrong I am to be in it?" Laurie held her breath. She hadn't

The Call of Duty

meant to make her mother cry, but she didn't want the wall she felt building up to come between them either.

"Y-yes." Her mother's tear-filled voice made her heart wrench. "I'm sorry."

"It's okay, Mom. I'm going to let you go so I can get home and hug you, okay?"

"I'd like that," her mom replied.

Relief filled her at her mom's words. "Good. Bye, Mom, I love you."

"Love you too Laurie. See you in a bit."

Laurie pushed the end button and pressed her hand to her forehead as she tried to control her emotions. This conversation had been a long time coming and she was glad it hadn't exploded as badly as it could have.

"Hey, you all right?"

She raised her head and placed a smile on her face as she nodded at Patrick. "Yeah, great. Everything's good. You ready?"

He raised an eyebrow at her and she realized he wasn't buying her lie. "Now, I may not know much, but I know a phone fight when I hear one. You wanna talk about it?"

"I..." Did she? Was she willing to tell him all of what her and her mother had just discussed? *Perhaps now is the perfect opportunity to be upfront with him too.* Motivated by the thought and by the argument she'd just had with her mother, Laurie sat down on the hood of her Monte, nodding her head.

"Okay, good. That's good. Is your mom mad I'm coming? I can stay here if it would be better." He closed the distance between them and took her hand.

"No, no, it's not that." Laurie chuckled, though it sounded hollow even to her own ears. "She's happy about you—very happy. It's just you weren't the solution she was hoping for."

Patrick tilted his head at her words. "Meaning?"

"She thought that being in a relationship would be the ticket to get me out of the military. Patrick, I like you. I like you a lot. Hell, I could see a real future with you, but the military is part of who I am. One day, when I'm ready, I'll get out. Right now though, I'm happy in it." She paused before giving his hand a squeeze. "Are...are you okay with that?"

Patrick squeezed her hand back and smiled at her. "You know, before you, I hadn't had a date since prom in high school. I stay so busy with this shop that I don't have time to date. You were the first person I met that I *made* the time for. How far away from here are you based?"

"Uh, about two and a half hours?" She fought the sick feeling that was now settling in her stomach again. It hadn't occurred to her that they wouldn't be able to go on regular dates like people who lived in the same city.

"That's not far, we can do this. Hey…" Patrick cupped her chin with his free hand and guided her gaze to his face. "We can do this. We can take turns driving to spend the weekend with the other every couple of weeks or however your schedule allows. You aren't so far away that we can't ever see each other. We can talk on the phone every day. The shop here will keep me out of trouble when I'm not with you, and I swear to you I'm not the kind of guy that's going to be looking at other women. Usually all I ever see is men anyway. Ugly men at that."

Despite her worries, she smiled at him. "No gearhead chicks?"

The expression on his face turned grim. "They are a rare species." As she laughed, Patrick stepped between her legs and kissed her forehead. "Which is why," he continued, "I won't be so willing to let you go. You are a diamond amongst the coal—unique, beautiful, and my treasured find."

Laurie leaned up and kissed him. *Could this man be any more perfect for me?* He released her hand and chin and wrapped his arms around her, his fingers kneading the small of her back.

"You might want to be careful, my coveralls are dirty," he murmured against her mouth.

"I like dirty," she replied, grinning at him.

He pulled back slightly and raised his brow at her. "Laurie, a good old home-grown girl like you isn't supposed to say things like that. I'm appalled."

"No you aren't, you are a Patrick," she teased. "And Patrick is very intrigued, so don't go pretending you aren't."

He kissed her again, this time with a depth and passion that had been absent since last night. "Know what I've always wanted to do?"

She shook her head, delighting in the sensation of her lips brushing his. "No. What?"

"I've always wanted to have sex with someone on the hood of a classic car." He grinned at her with mischievous sparkle in his eyes.

She gasped. "You too?"

Secret Cravings Publishing
www.secretcravingspublishing.com